It Was A Fantastic Sensation,

Jess thought, half dazed. To think he had planned to keep sex on more or less casual terms—an easy, comfortable basis that would satisfy each of them physically but not demand too much emotionally. He knew it was possible to enjoy a physical relationship on that level, but God help him, he would have missed so much if he'd succeeded in doing that with Elly.

It wasn't until tonight, when she had begged him to make love to her, that Jess had finally acknowledged that the sexual relationship with Elly wasn't going to be casual at all. Her own need and passion were pulling him into the heart of a whirlwind.

There was no aphrodisiac on earth that could compare to being wanted the way Elly seemed to want him tonight.

Dear Reader,

Welcome to Silhouette! Our goal is to give you hours of unbeatable reading pleasure, and we hope you'll enjoy each month's six new Silhouette Desires. These sensual, provocative love stories are both believable and compelling—sometimes they're poignant, sometimes humorous, but always enjoyable.

Indulge yourself. Experience all the passion and excitement of falling in love along with our heroine as she meets the irresistible man of her dreams and together they overcome all obstacles in the path to a happy ending.

If this is your first Desire, I hope it'll be the first of many. If you're already a Silhouette Desire reader, thanks for your support! Look for some of your favorite authors in the coming months: Stephanie James, Diana Palmer, Dixie Browning, Ann Major and Doreen Owens Malek, to name just a few.

Happy reading!

Isabel Swift
Senior Editor

STEPHANIE JAMES
Cautious Lover

Silhouette Desire

Published by Silhouette Books New York

America's Publisher of Contemporary Romance

SILHOUETTE BOOKS
300 E. 42nd St., New York, N.Y. 10017

Copyright © 1986 by Jayne Krentz, Inc.

Distributed by Pocket Books

ISBN: 0-373-05253-7

First Silhouette Books printing January 1986

10 9 8 7 6 5 4 3 2 1

America's Publisher of Contemporary Romance

Printed in the U.S.A.

STEPHANIE JAMES

readily admits that the chief influence on her writing is her "lifelong addiction to romantic daydreaming." She has spent the past nine years living and working with her engineer husband in a wide variety of places, including the Caribbean, the Southeast and the Pacific Northwest. Ms. James currently resides in Washington.

One

It hadn't been the most romantic proposal of marriage a woman had ever received. If Elly Trent wasn't so passionately in love with Jess Winter, she knew she would have told him exactly what he could do with his suggestion of marriage. Here on the Oregon coast there were several points where he could take himself and his offer for a long walk off a short cliff. In the depths of her initial disappointment, Elly would have been happy to show him the way.

But she had recovered quickly and done the only logical thing under the circumstances. She'd asked for time to think it over. She had stalled him now for a week and Jess wasn't an easy man to stall. He always seemed to be operating on some internal master plan, a schedule that he adhered to strictly. When you found yourself on his schedule, as Elly had, you soon learned you were expected to fall into place on time and on-line.

There were other reasons for not fighting the schedule. Lately Elly had become more and more aware of a curious reluctance on her part to push Jess too hard. There was something about him that warned her he was not a man to be prodded in any direction other than the one he himself chose to go. A part of her feared what would happen if she tried it. She couldn't bear the thought of losing him.

The offer of marriage had come last weekend. On Sunday evening, as usual, Jess had returned to Portland, where he spent his time as a very expensive, very high-powered and occasionally very ruthless executive consultant. Elly had never actually witnessed the ruthless side of him, but she didn't doubt for a moment that side existed. She knew from experience that a man didn't become as successful in the corporate world as Jess had been if he wasn't capable of doing a little bloodletting.

He'd reappeared this afternoon, just as he always did on Friday afternoons, pacing into her shop, The Natural Choice, with that strong, controlled stride that said so much about his basic nature. He was on time, of course. Jess was always on time.

Elly had looked up from behind the cash register, where she'd been ringing up a pound of whole-wheat flour together with two dozen granola bars and known that she wasn't going to be able to stall anything for another week. He was a reasonably patient, unflappable, coolly mannered man, but he was also calmly persistent. One look into his fog-gray eyes had been enough to tell Elly that the issue between them would be settled one way or another this weekend. She didn't need a second look to know that Jess fully expected the matter to be resolved the way he wanted it.

Now she stood in her kitchen, her mind whirling with uncertainty about the bold plans she had hatched during the long week. Elly opened the oven door and peered at the simmering lentil casserole inside. She had closed her shop an hour earlier and then invited Jess home for dinner. The invitation itself was fairly routine. She'd cooked dinner for him often enough on weekends during the past two months.

But tonight was not going to be routine. She'd made her decision. All she needed now was the courage to implement the test. She leaned over to probe the surface of the casserole.

"*Ouch! Dammit....*" Muttering disgustedly, Elly turned on the cold-water faucet and stuck her finger beneath the spray.

"What happened?" Jess wandered into the spacious old kitchen cradling a glass of Scotch in one hand. He stood frowning in the doorway, his free hand braced easily against the wooden frame.

"Nothing. Burned my finger, that's all. The casserole's hot."

"I'll bet." He smiled briefly. "Are you okay? Want me to drag out the first-aid kit?"

Elly shook her head, turning off the water. "No, I'm fine. Really." She picked up the loaf of dark, whole-grain bread that was sitting on the counter and reached for a knife. Behind her she could feel him studying her quick, tense movements.

"Be careful with that knife, Elly. I just sharpened it last week. You're used to working with dull blades."

"I know. Thursday I cut myself on the paring knife. I didn't realize you'd sharpened that one, too."

"I had to sharpen it," he told her reproachfully. "You'd been using it to dig around in the dirt again."

"I'd just used it to trim a few leaves off my ivy plants." She defended herself with a placating smile, hoping Jess wouldn't go into the subject too deeply.

He gave her an indulgent look. "Like hell. That blade had been dulled almost past redemption. You'd used it for more than whacking off a couple of leaves."

Elly coughed to clear her throat. "Yes, well, it's very useful around the plants."

"And you've got a house full of plants." Jess reached out to finger the leaves of the huge, bushy fern hung nearby. "You should use proper gardening tools, though, Elly. Not your good kitchen knives. You never know when you're going to need a good, sharp knife."

"Yes, I know." She concentrated on the bread. With any luck the bread knife would do its job properly and not betray the fact that she had used it last Friday to cut away a cardboard container that held a new plant she had purchased.

"Everything go all right at the shop this week?" Ice clinked as Jess raised the glass of Scotch to his mouth.

"Fine, just fine." She piled the thick slices of bread on a plate. "What about you? Going to be able to wind up your consulting job on schedule?"

"Yes."

Elly put down her knife and picked up the glass of Pinot Noir she'd been sipping. "Yes," she repeated thoughtfully. "Of course. Why not? You always get things done on schedule, don't you?"

Jess tilted his head slightly to one side, considering the woman in front of him. His gaze wandered over the neat coronet of braided chestnut-colored hair, took in the warm, tawny-gold eyes and the brilliant persimmon-colored sweater Elly was wearing over a pair of snug, faded jeans. The sweater was loose, not revealing the gentle swell of small, high-tipped breasts. The jeans, on the other hand, clearly outlined the flare of curving thighs. She was slightly flushed from the heat of the stove, and she looked very good to him. He wondered at the faint edge in her voice.

"Why are you nervous tonight, honey?" Jess came forward to lean against the kitchen counter. He lifted the same hand in which he held the glass of Scotch and touched her jaw with one blunt-tipped finger. "Why so sharp? You're usually so easy and restful to come back to on the weekends, but this afternoon you've been as tense as a drawn bow. Are you sure you're not having trouble at the shop?"

The glass of Scotch was so close to her face that Elly could feel the coolness coming from it. She looked up at Jess and smiled tremulously. "We're not all as calm and collected as you are, Jess."

He smiled abruptly, the expression momentarily easing the harsh, grim planes of his face. Elly's first impression of Jess Winter was that he fit in perfectly with the rugged landscape that characterized the local coastline. Nothing she had learned about him in the past two months had changed her initial reaction. There was little conventional attractiveness about the man, but for her there was a compelling element of strength and vitality beneath the quiet exterior. It was there, she was sure, both mentally and physically. The physical part showed in the solid, lean lines of his body.

Jess Winter, she knew, was thirty-seven years old. He had spent those years making himself successful, and Elly suspected that he'd made it on his own terms. There was too much raw power and passion lying just beneath the surface of the man to allow him to take the easy way out of any situation in which he might find himself. She just wished some of that passion she sensed in him could be channeled in her direction.

Until now her relationship with Jess Winter had been the epitome of a polite, friendly, all-too-casual courtship. He came to her on the weekends seeking peace and quiet, not excitement and passion. If Elly's instincts hadn't warned her that there was a vein of fire to be tapped in this man she would have given up in frustration several weeks ago. As it was she might have to face the fact that she simply wasn't the woman who could bring out the passionate side of his nature.

In certain very specific ways, she reflected grimly, Jess Winter lived up to his name. At least with her. She had wondered from time to time if there had been other women in his life who had been fortunate enough to know the full depths of this man. She didn't want to speculate too long on the subject. It was depressing.

"You're nervous because you're about to accept an offer of marriage," Jess said with characteristic insight. Amusement lit his eyes. "That's it, isn't it? You know that sometime this weekend you're going to have to stop dwelling on the matter and simply say yes. The funny part is I didn't expect the whole thing to set you on edge like this."

"Well, it certainly doesn't seem to have set you on edge," Elly muttered tartly.

Jess shrugged. "Why should it? We both know we're doing the right thing."

"Do we?"

"Elly, we're perfect for each other and you know it. You're just what I need. Just what I want."

Elly busied herself putting the bread into the oven to warm. It was easier than meeting his eyes. "Are you sure, Jess? Are you really sure you know what you're doing?"

"Is that what's worrying you? That I don't know my own mind? After the past eight weeks you should know me better than that."

Elly sighed as she closed the oven door. "You're right. I should know you better than that. You always seem to be aware of exactly what you're doing and why. The way you arrived in town two months ago and immediately began negotiating for that old Victorian monstrosity on the bluff overlooking the sea, the way you're deliberately winding down your career as a consultant so that you can move here and set up an inn, *everything* you do. It's all neat and tidy and certain." She shook her head and reached for her glass of wine again. "You seem to have all the little loose ends of your life neatly tied off."

"I've been working on it," he reminded her softly.

Elly took a long sip of the wine. "I realize that."

"Getting things in order, tying off loose ends, knowing what I want and how to get it, those are my strong suits, Elly. That's the way I operate. I didn't think it bothered you."

Instantly she heard herself rush in to reassure him. "It doesn't bother me! I admire you for the way you're taking the risk of starting a whole new career. I admire the way you get things done. You've got so many plans and ideas, and I just know you'll be successful running your inn, but I'm—" She broke off in frustration, unable to put her real fears into words.

"You're what, Elly?"

"I guess I'm just not sure why you want to marry me," she concluded lamely. "I know this sounds trite, but frankly, I wouldn't have thought I was your type."

"Ah, I see."

"Well, I'm glad somebody does!"

Jess grinned. "What kind of woman do you think would be my type?"

Elly stared stonily across the kitchen, concentrating on the row of African violet plants she had sitting on the windowsill. "Someone a little flashier than me; no, a *lot* flashier than me. Someone with a high-powered career in the city, perhaps. A fashion model, a lawyer or a corporate executive, maybe. Someone who knows clothes and the right people. Someone with style and wit and flair."

"You're describing exactly the kind of woman I don't want." Amusement underlay his words. "Besides, what would I do out here on the coast with a high-powered lady executive who was into clothes and Porsches and high-tech furniture? That kind of creature needs a city environment. She'd give me nothing but trouble here. Too much trouble."

"And you think I won't?" Elly dared.

Jess laughed and reached out playfully to grab a handful of her neatly bound braids. He gave her a light shake that rumpled her hair but didn't dislodge the coronet. "The only trouble you're likely to give me is starving me to death. When do we eat?"

"You're avoiding the question."

"No, I'm not. There isn't any question to be avoided." He leaned down and brushed a kiss across the tip of her nose. "I keep telling you, we're perfect for each other. We're—" he searched for the word "—comfortable together. Similar interests, similar tastes, similar goals. As soon as I complete my move from Portland, we're going to share similar life-styles. We both like this little town with its Victorian monstrosities. Just look at this place you call home!"

Elly ignored the reference to the old, weather-beaten two-story house she had bought two years ago. She wouldn't let herself be sidetracked. "Has it occurred to you that I may not see myself in the role of comfortable companion?"

Some of the affectionate humor faded in Jess as he eyed her challenging expression. "Are you sure nothing is wrong, Elly?"

"Of course I'm sure."

"You're not acting normally."

"You mean I'm not proving very comfortable this evening?"

"Easy, honey," he said soothingly. "As long as you're just tense because you're on the verge of getting married, I won't worry about it."

"What would you worry about?"

He lifted one shoulder casually. "If there was something more serious bothering you, I'd be concerned."

"Really? What would you do about it?" She couldn't seem to stop herself from deliberately pressing the issue. It was ridiculous. There was nothing to be gained from this approach. Besides, this wasn't the way she had planned to have the evening develop.

He looked at her oddly. "I'd do whatever had to be done," he said simply.

Elly closed her eyes in brief frustration. This was getting her nowhere. "Forget it, Jess. I don't know why I'm spitting at you. It's just that I've been thinking about you all week, knowing you'd expect an answer this weekend. I've been getting more and more anxious for no real reason." She tried a fragile grin. "After all, what can you expect under the circumstances? Women my age aren't accustomed to receiving offers of marriage every day of the week."

"Thirty is fairly advanced, all right. You should be grateful I've come along to rescue you from a life of boring spinsterhood." There was wicked laughter in his eyes.

."Is that how you see yourself? As my rescuer?"

"To tell you the truth," Jess said mildly, "I think the opposite is the case. You're rescuing me."

That caught her interest. "From what?"

"More than you will ever know," he said lightly, dismissing the subject with a casual wave of a hand. Isn't that casserole ready yet?"

Elly decided she could take a hint when she got hit over the head with it. "I think so. Why don't you take the bottle of wine over to the table?" She turned back to the stove, occupying herself with ladle and bowls.

He teased her about saving her from spinsterhood, but the unnerving truth was that Jess Winter had made no real effort to introduce any degree of passion into the relationship. Some salvation, she thought wryly. The light kiss with which he had dusted her nose a few minutes ago was typical of the caresses Elly had received from him in the past two months. She thought about it bleakly as she ladled the rich lentil concoction into earthenware bowls and heaped grated romano cheese on top of it.

There had been casual hugs, pleasantly warm but almost cautious embraces, a great deal of hand-holding and one or two kisses that Elly thought contained the seeds of passion. Frustratingly, those seeds had not been allowed to grow. It seemed to her that as soon as Jess sensed any threat to his self-control he pulled back. It was not only odd in this day and age to have a man approach an essentially sensual relationship so carefully, it was downright disturbing. After all, Elly told herself worriedly, it wasn't as if they were teenagers who were sneaking around behind the barn. In fact, teenagers, under the circumstances, probably would have had more fun. And womanly instinct told her that Jess Winter definitely was interested in women. So why hadn't he pushed her into bed by now? He certainly wouldn't have had to push very hard. The thought that he might not be attracted to her was terrifying. It also made no sense. Why would he want to marry her if he wasn't attracted to her?

Her only hope had been the occasional glimpses of fire she thought she had detected on the few times when Jess had permitted a good-night embrace to stray beyond the bounds he usually imposed. She thought she had sensed something more in him on those infrequent occasions, something that meant he was capable of responding to her deeply. Those hints of passion, combined with her instinctive reading of his character, were all she had to go on tonight. If she couldn't find a way to test the sensual side of his nature, Elly knew she would be forced to decline Jess Winter's offer of marriage. It would be too big a risk.

She might be thirty, but she hadn't reached the point of desperation and probably never would. She wasn't ready to commit herself to marriage simply to avoid spinsterhood. As a matter of fact, there was a lot to be said for living independently. She had grown quite fond of her freedom and her own company. Only love would coax her into marriage—fully reciprocated love. Elly had made that decision this morning.

"How long will you be staying this time?" she asked as she carried the bowls over to the round wooden table by the window. She returned to the oven to collect the rest of the meal.

Jess shook his head in mock wonder. "You're always so calm and serene about that particular question. A lot of women would have given me a great deal of static over the matter of my coming and going so frequently. But not you.'' He reached for a hot bowl. ''You always smile and kiss me goodbye when I leave and invariably you're waiting right where I left you when I return.''

''I had no idea I was so convenient.'' Elly sat down and concentrated on tasting her casserole.

''Ah, but you are convenient, Elly. Undemanding, good-natured, genuine, reliable, tolerant and you can cook. What more could a man ask?''

She sighed, her mouth curving wryly. ''You're teasing me.''

''You're asking for it.'' Jess's eyes gleamed. ''But to tell you the truth, all those perfect female qualities I just listed aren't so far from reality. You do possess them.''

''And you're a man who appreciates them?''

''You better believe it.''

The depressing thing was, he clearly meant it. The rather daunting list of dull virtues was exactly what Jess did seem to admire in her. After two months Elly believed him. The thought nearly panicked her.

''What if I turned out to be not quite so, uh, comfortable?'' she dared softly.

Jess grinned. ''It's really starting to get to you, isn't it?''

''What?''

''Bridal jitters.''

''I'm not a bride yet,'' she pointed out coolly.

He leaned across the table and flicked the end of her short nose. It was a gesture of casual affection, just as all his other gestures were. ''You're going to make a charming bride. Now stop worrying about it and pass me the salad.''

Without a word Elly obeyed. The time had come, she thought. It was now or never. She had to start focusing the evening toward her ultimate goal or the opportunity would be lost. Deliberately she summoned up a sweet smile. "You can't blame me for being nervous. I've never been married before."

"You'll get the hang of it fast enough. All you have to do is keep living your life the way you normally live it. The only difference is that I'll be around to share it with you."

"Sounds simple."

"It will be. Want some more salad?" He dished out a large portion for her without bothering to wait for her response.

"No, thank you."

"Too late. It's already on your plate. That dressing's terrific, by the way. Invent it yourself?"

"Um-hmm."

"You know, I think that after we're married I'll move in here with you while we wait for the renovation work on the inn," he went on casually. "When it's finished we can live there."

"Jess—"

"I'm almost finished winding things up in Portland. I figure another couple of weeks and I'll be through entirely. If we plan the wedding for the end of the month everything should dovetail nicely. All right with you?"

"Jess, I think we ought to discuss this."

"There's nothing major to discuss. I'll handle all the details. Just decide how many of your local laid-back artsy-craftsy friends you want to invite to the wedding. We can have the reception right here, I think. Should be enough room."

Elly gave up trying to deflect him from his casual planning of her life. Instead she tried to make the appropriate responses even though she was growing increasingly tense. She'd never set out deliberately to seduce a man before, and the prospect was intimidating. It would have been much simpler if she'd been certain of the reception she was likely to receive. But with Jess Winter there was no predicting the outcome.

"Leave the dishes," she said quickly as they finished the meal. Jess had started to clear the table the way he usually did. Elly smiled tremulously as she got to her feet. "We can do them later."

He nodded. "Okay. Whatever you like."

She cleared her throat, aware of the quickening of adrenaline in her body. "I thought it might be nice to build a fire and have a glass of brandy in front of it. How does that sound?" She was already leading the way into the living room, allowing him little option but to follow.

"Sounds fine."

Jess walked over to the old stone hearth and went down on one knee in front of it. He reached for the kindling Elly had piled in the brass wood basket.

"There is some newspaper in that sack," Elly said as she tried unobtrusively to turn off some of the lights. "You can use it to start the fire."

"Newspaper and something else." He peered into the sack. "What's this? Mail?" He pulled out an envelope addressed to her and held it up inquiringly.

"That's okay. Just a letter from my cousin. I've already read it. I toss most of my papers into that sack so I'll always have something with which to start a fire."

Jess nodded, striking a match and setting the flame to the edge of the envelope. When the paper caught fire he used it to light the kindling. "How much family do you have besides this cousin?"

"The usual assortment, I guess. I don't have any brothers or sisters, though. My parents are retired and live back East. They're on an extended cruise at the moment. The rest of my relatives live in California. That includes Dave's parents.''

"Dave?''

"The cousin who wrote me that letter," Elly explained as she gazed thoughtfully around the darkened room. Jess hadn't seemed to notice that she was trying to produce a romantic glow.

"He lives in California?''

"No, he's in college in Seattle.''

She didn't particularly want to discuss Dave just then. She had other things on her mind. She eyed Jess as he concentrated on his fire. The glow of the flames was beginning to cast a warm tone over the atmosphere of the room, just as she had hoped. In the firelight she could see hints of the silver in Jess's dark hair. There was a casual, thoroughly masculine grace about him as he knelt in front of the flames. She responded to it the way she always did, wanting to touch him. Elly dug her nails into her palms in agony over the suspense and tension. Then she drew a deep breath and forced herself to relax.

"How was the drive from Portland?'' she asked blandly as she walked over to an oak end table and poured two brandies.

"No problem. The fog's coming in tonight, though. I'm glad I got here before dark.'' Jess got to his feet and accepted the snifter from her with a smile.

"Sit down.'' Elly graciously indicated the depths of the huge, overstuffed sofa. When he'd obligingly seated himself she sank down beside him, curling her legs under and leaning into him to feel his warmth. Jess's arm slipped automatically around her shoulders, and he took a thoughtful sip of brandy. She could feel him relaxing.

"Honey, you don't know how good this is," he murmured. "All week I look forward to getting back here and unwinding with you."

"I'm glad."

"So tell me what you've been doing this past week," Jess invited lazily.

"Not much. Just the usual." Elly tried to nestle closer. It seemed to her that Jess's arm tightened fractionally but not much. He seemed content to sit like this for the rest of the evening. "We lead a very quiet life around here during the winter, Jess." She took a breath. "Are you sure it's not going to be too quiet for you?"

"I know what I'm doing, Elly. I usually do."

She inclined her head, staring into the flames. "I believe you. I just wish I knew what I was doing."

"Stop worrying and leave everything to me." He lifted his hand to toy with her braids.

Elly waited hopefully, but his touch was clearly just another absent caress, not the prelude to taking down her hair. She sighed inwardly, knowing that if she didn't take the initiative, they would sit here all evening like this. Deliberately Elly put her fingertips on Jess's thigh. Jess didn't seem to notice. Elly took another swallow of brandy to fortify herself.

"You were right about the fog," she said, a little startled that the words sounded so husky in her throat. "It's very heavy tonight."

"Umm." Jess leaned his head back against the cushions, his eyes closing in obvious contentment.

"It makes things cozy, don't you think?" Good grief. If he fell asleep on her she would know for certain there was no hope of any passion in the forthcoming marriage. Nervously Elly began drawing tiny patterns on

Jess's thigh. Through the fabric of his well-tailored slacks she could feel the heat of his body.

"Cozy? I hadn't thought of it that way, but I suppose it does. During the winter months we'll have to promote the inn as a quiet, cozy retreat. A place far away from the hustle of the city."

"Romantic," Elly suggested tentatively. "You could promote it as a romantic hideaway on a windswept coast. Doesn't that sound appropriate?"

"Maybe I should let you handle the advertising," he said with a trace of humor.

"Maybe you should." She took a deep breath, her fingers tightening around her glass. Then she let her hand slide down along the inside of his leg. Simultaneously she turned her face into his chest. It was obvious she was going to have to be more aggressive. "You smell good."

"Not likely. I haven't showered since this morning." Jess still sounded incredibly unconcerned.

He stirred faintly, though, just enough to let Elly know that he wasn't completely unaware of her physically. Encouraged, she put her glass down on the table at the end of the sofa, leaning intimately across Jess as she did so. When she finished the small task, she took advantage of her position to increase the closeness between them. She put her hand on the first button of his shirt.

"No, really, you do smell good," she insisted, resting her cheek on his shoulder as she fiddled with the button. "Warm and sexy."

"I had no idea what a lack of a shower could do for a man," Jess said dryly. He shifted a little. She couldn't tell if he was trying to put more distance between them or if he was just restless. "Easy honey. I don't want to spill this good brandy."

"There's plenty more where that came from." She succeeded in undoing the button at last. Her fingers strayed inside the opening of his white shirt. Elly caught her breath as she felt the crisp, curly hair. Impulsively she turned her head and put her lips to the base of his throat.

"Elly, honey—"

"I've missed you this week, Jess." She kissed him again, this time on his jaw. Her fingers slipped around his neck.

"I missed you, too," he whispered.

Elly thought she heard him sigh softly into her hair. Emboldened, she leaned more heavily into him, letting him feel the shape of her soft, unconfined breasts on his hard chest. His fingers tightened on her shoulder, and now she was sure he was no longer quite so relaxed. She could feel his body tightening as she snuggled against him.

"I've done a lot of thinking this week, Jess."

"Have you?" His hand lifted to her hair again, and this time he removed a couple of pins.

"There are some things we've never talked about," she ventured, closing her eyes as she felt her hair coming free.

"And you've been worrying about them?"

"Yes."

"Elly, honey, there's no need to worry. We've got all the time in the world. There's no rush. Everything's on schedule."

"I know that, but—" She broke off, unable to put her fears into words. Instead she clung to him, abruptly digging her fingertips into his shoulders. A little desperately she found his mouth with her own, praying for a response.

At first there was only the polite, warm, agreeable reaction of a man who knows what's expected of him under the circumstances and is willing to oblige.

But Elly had had enough of his polite, obliging kisses during the past two months. Tonight she needed to know that his feelings for her went deeper. She had to find out just what he felt for her. Her whole future depended on the answer. Inching her way appealingly into Jess's lap, she curled against him and opened her mouth invitingly beneath his. Her desire was naked now, leaving her totally vulnerable.

Elly felt the hesitation in Jess and could have wept. Then, just as she was convinced that he felt nothing for her—at least nothing he would admit to—Jess slowly began to respond.

The very fact that he seemed to be fighting his own response flooded Elly with hope. She moaned softly against his mouth, a wordless plea that was also an unwitting, very feminine form of seduction. Then she caught his hand in one of her own. Trembling, she guided his fingers under the edge of her sweater.

Jess sucked in his breath. Beneath her thigh Elly was now unmistakably aware of his growing arousal. Shivering with nervous relief and an even more nervous exhilaration, she urged his hand higher.

"Please, Jess. Please touch me. I—I need you. I want you to need me." The words were breathless pleas against Jess's throat as Elly trembled in his arms.

Jess groaned. "Elly, honey, I didn't plan it to be like this."

"But, Jess, this is the way it's supposed to be," she whispered desperately. "Make love to me, Jess. Please make love to me. I'm begging you."

"Oh, God, Elly. I don't—I didn't want—You don't know what you're asking."

But his hand closed over her breasts with a sensual possessiveness Elly had never known in him before. The last of her doubts faded as she felt the undeniable impact of the first deeply sexual contact she'd ever had with Jess Winter. He did want her. The fire she had sensed in him really did exist.

Elly almost sobbed in relief, and then she felt the room shift on its axis as Jess lowered her onto the sofa cushions. A moment later he came down on top of her. The firelight clearly revealed the masculine hunger that was at last beginning to etch his face.

Two

It was going to be all right, Jess thought as the need in him flared into heavy and demanding life. There had been nothing to worry about after all. And to think he'd been deliberately putting off this end of things. What a fool. *It was going to be all right.*

No, it was going to be better than all right. He realized that as Elly began to cling to him with increasing passion. She was so soft and hot, her tawny-gold eyes full of a totally honest plea. She wanted him. The desire in her was not a false spell she wove to ensnare him. It was genuine, completely genuine. It made her so sweetly vulnerable.

Beneath him Jess could feel the gentle swell of Elly's breasts. The need to see and touch her small, excitingly hard nipples came over him in a rush. With an awkward urgency that astonished him, he pulled the persimmon sweater up over her head, letting the garment drop to the floor. He inhaled fiercely as the fire's glow spilled over her bare breasts.

"Ah, Elly, my sweet Elly. You're so lovely."

She shivered as he carefully brushed his thumb across one thrusting peak. Her reaction to his touch heightened Jess's excitement as nothing else could have. He lifted his head and saw that her eyes were half-closed against the exquisite need building up in her. Along the length of his leg her jeaned thigh tightened, her knee flexing slightly.

It was a fantastic sensation, Jess thought, half-dazed. To think he had planned to keep sex on more or less casual terms, an easy, comfortable basis that would satisfy each of them physically but not demand too much emotionally. He knew it was possible to enjoy a physical relationship on that level because he'd had more than one such association since Marina had left. But, God help him, he would have missed so much if he'd succeeded in doing that with Elly.

It wasn't until tonight, when she had begged him to make love to her, that Jess had finally acknowledged that the sexual relationship with Elly wasn't going to be casual. Her own need and passion were pulling him into the heart of a whirlwind. There was no aphrodisiac on earth that could compare to being wanted the way Elly seemed to want him tonight.

Elly didn't know which was stronger, the dizzy sensation of relief and exultation or the flaring physical excitement. In the end it didn't matter. She was aware she had fallen in love with Jess Winter, but she'd had no real notion of the depths of the physical side of the matter. It was glorious, the most incredible sensation she'd ever known.

She felt the hard readiness of Jess's body through the fabric of her jeans. He had his shirt off now and the strong, sleek slopes of his shoulders were golden in the firelight. He crushed her deeply into the sofa cushions, his fingers lancing through her hair. The last of the pins came free, and Jess muttered something dark and sensuous. He nipped passionately at the line of her throat.

"Your hair has fire in it," he told her wonderingly. Catching a long tendril of the chestnut-colored stuff he curled the end around one nipple. The teasing caress elicited another soft sound from Elly. Jess seemed enthralled with her reaction.

"Jess, I've been so worried," Elly confided huskily as she tightened her arms around his neck. "I was afraid you didn't want me."

"That's the last thing you have to worry about now." He found her mouth with his own, kissing her with drugging desire.

Elly sighed and gave herself up to the passionate excitement that swirled around her. Loving Jess was going to be all she could have hoped. She was certain of that now.

And then, without any warning, Elly's fiery world of love and passion froze into a solid sheet of ice. Lost in the shimmering moment, it took several timeless seconds before she realized that Jess had gone utterly still above her.

"*Marina*!" The name was a thick, muffled sound seemingly wrenched from his throat. "Damn it to hell. *Marina*!"

"What is it? Jess? What's wrong?" Dazed by the sudden turn of events, Elly opened her eyes to see the savagely drawn features of the man who had only a moment before been making love to her. Jess was staring past her toward the living-room window. She swallowed and started to ask another question, but before she could get the confused words out of her mouth, he was pulling himself free of her.

"Jess!" Panicked by the change in him, Elly struggled to a sitting position. She felt suddenly cold and vulnerable without her sweater. Instinctively she crossed her arms over her breasts.

But Jess wasn't paying any attention to her. He was already halfway across the room, racing toward the undraped window. Reaching it, he unlatched the frame and shoved open the glass. The muscles of his back tightened with the swift movement. The chill fog that had been hovering outside seemed to slide eagerly into the cozy room.

"Jess, where are you going?" Horrified, Elly sprang to her feet as Jess swung first one leg and then the other over the windowsill. A moment later he disappeared into the night. She stood staring after him, the back of her hand held to her mouth in a timeless gesture of fear and incomprehension.

Time ticked past. Through the open window the cold night air continued to pour hungrily into the room, devouring the warmth it found there. The fire in front of the hearth tried to beat back at the attacking chill, but it was already beginning to flicker beneath the onslaught.

Elly shook off the mesmerizing effects of her anxiety and started toward the window. Vaguely she realized it ought to be closed before any more cold air came into the room. As she took a step forward, her toe snagged on her sweater. Hastily she bent down and retrieved it, shrugging into it quickly.

The window got stuck, as it nearly always did, and Elly was obliged to exert her full strength to get it closed and latched. With the deed accomplished she sagged against the sill and stared out into the darkness. Nothing was visible through the fog.

Unable to think of anything more productive to do, Elly continued to stare out the window. Her chaotic thoughts gradually settled back into place, and at last she began to think clearly again.

What had Jess seen that had sent him into the night? Prowlers? But you rarely called a prowler by name.

Marina. It was a name, Elly realized. A woman's name. She shivered, but this time the involuntary reaction wasn't caused by sensual tension.

Elly was still standing at the window when the door behind her opened. Eyes widening with fear, she whirled to find Jess on the threshold. His naked chest was damp, whether from exertion or the fog, she couldn't tell. Across the room his wintry eyes met hers, and Elly knew she was looking at a man who had metamorphosed from lover to stranger. Her hand curled into a small, tense fist at her side. She tried to speak, failed and began again.

"What happened, Jess? For God's sake, tell me what happened! Did you see someone outside the window?"

He broke the eye contact, turning to shut the door and lock it with deliberate care. When he turned back, Elly could see a coldness in his gaze that matched the night. Her fear rose another notch. Something in her expression must have gotten through to him. Jess frowned and started forward. He stopped when she instinctively backed up a pace.

"It's all right, Elly. I'm sorry I scared you."

"What did you see?"

He ran the back of his hand across his eyes in a weary gesture. "A face. I thought I saw someone standing on the other side of the window. But when I got outside I couldn't find a thing." His hand dropped from his face.

"Not surprising. Godzilla could be hiding out there in that pea soup, and I wouldn't be able to see him."

"If you saw a prowler I should call Charlie." Elly reached for the phone.

"Charlie? Oh, yeah. The local deputy sheriff. Forget it, Elly. You can't see two feet in front of yourself tonight. By the time Charlie made it here through the fog, whoever was out there will be long gone. Hell, whoever it was is long gone now." Jess paced over to an armchair and dropped into it with a deep sigh. He stared broodingly into the flames.

Behind him Elly let the phone drop back into the cradle. She stayed very still, watching the stranger who had invaded her living room. Whoever he was, he wasn't the same man she had come to know during the past two months. The realization was frightening. A part of her urged flight. But another side of her demanded explanations.

"Jess, who did you think it was outside the window?"

He didn't move. There was along silence before he answered. "A woman."

Elly drew a deep, steadying breath. "You called her name."

"Did I?"

"You called her Marina."

He didn't respond to that. His whole attention was fixed on the fire. Slowly Elly moved closer to his chair. Her hands were shaking.

"Jess?"

"I'm sorry, Elly."

She shook her head bewilderedly. "Who is Marina?"

It was a while before he answered her, and when he did Elly got the feeling Jess was trying to convince himself as much as her. "I didn't see Marina outside that window. Just someone who looked like her."

Elly licked her lower lip. She felt as if she were walking on very thin ice. Beneath the fragile surface, endless cold waited to swallow her whole. "What does Marina look like?"

Jess rested his chin on his fist, propping his elbow on the upholstered arm of the chair. "A witch," he finally said very succinctly. "A blond-haired, green-eyed witch."

Elly closed her eyes. "I see."

"No, you don't. You can't possibly."

Her lashes lifted, and she stared again at his hard fire-lit profile. She asked the next question because she had no alternative. The need to know the truth was greater than the fear and hopelessness it might bring. "Who was Marina, Jess?"

He hesitated a moment longer and then said very softly, "My ex-wife."

Elly had a hard time getting her next breath. When she finally got it, her voice sounded faint, even to her own ears. "I didn't realize you had been married."

"I'm thirty-seven years old, Elly. Most men have experimented at least once with marriage by the time they reach my age."

She sank down onto the couch, clasping her hands tightly in her lap. "Yes, I suppose they have. I just hadn't thought about it, I guess. It hadn't crossed my mind. You never mentioned—"

"It's not something I talk about."

"Obviously!" A profound silence followed that remark and then Elly asked tentatively, "Children?"

"Hell, no. I wouldn't have kept quiet about children, Elly."

"Just ex-wives?" A thread of anger was beginning to weave its way into her emotions.

"There was no need to mention Marina."

"Why not?"

"Because she's dead, Elly."

Elly closed her eyes in sudden anguish. "Oh, my God. And when you started to make love to me, *really* make love to me, you saw a vision of her at the window."

The words had the unexpected effect of snapping Jess out of his brooding state. Elly was completely unprepared for the way he surged out of the chair and swept across the room in three angry strides. His face was lined with controlled fury. Halting in front of her, Jess reached down to grasp her shoulders fiercely. His gray eyes seemed to pierce her with lances of ice.

"No," he bit out savagely, "I did not see a vision of her when I started to make love to you. I saw someone outside that window."

"Someone who looked just like her?" Elly said in a tight voice.

"Someone who looked a lot like her. But I sure as hell didn't see a vision. For crying out loud, Elly, what the hell do you think is going on?"

"You tell me. I can't seem to think straight. All I know is that one minute you're making love to me as if . . . as if you mean it finally, and the next you're seeing your ex-wife at the window. What do you expect me to think?"

"I expect you to be rational about it," Jess grated, hauling her to her feet in front of him. "There was someone outside that window who bore a resemblance to a woman I married and divorced a few years ago. That's all. In the morning I'll take a look around and see if I can find any signs of the prowler. Frankly, though, it's not likely."

"No," she admitted politely, letting him put any construction on her agreement that he might wish. Lifting her chin, she made an effort to evade his hands. "Well," she tried to say in a conversational tone, "it's getting late, isn't it? And it's going to be a slow drive back to your motel in this fog. You'd probably better get started. Give me a call in the morning. I'll be at the shop, as usual."

"Elly—"

"Did I mention that Bill Franklin was asking about you this week?" she continued as she went over to the hall closet and began pulling out Jess's worn leather jacket. "He said he's got the estimates on the plumbing work ready for you. You might want to look him up tomorrow. I gather his schedule is fairly open, though. Shouldn't be too much trouble figuring out when he can do the job...."

"Elly!" Jess came forward and yanked the jacket out of her hands, replacing it in the closet. "Stop chattering at me like that. I'm not driving anywhere in this damn fog. I couldn't see my way out to the car, let alone see the white line on the road."

Despairingly, Elly realized he was right. It had been her own agitation that had made her try to push him out of her home. The truth was she was trapped with him, perhaps until morning. Earlier the prospect had seemed an inviting one. Now it held only uncertainty and a nameless fear.

She had to get hold of herself. Taking a deep breath, Elly stalked across the room and picked up the brandy glass she had set down on the table beside the sofa. The fiery liquid trickling down her throat was a welcome and distinctly reviving sensation.

"I could use another drink, myself." Jess's voice was a low growl as he crossed the room and poured himself more brandy. He stood with his feet planted wide apart, one hand on his hips and downed a healthy swallow.

Elly eyed him covertly, thinking he looked very pagan. She wished he would put on his shirt. Belatedly she reached down and picked it up, handing it to him. "Here. You're probably cold from running around outside without any clothes on."

Surprisingly her grumbling comment brought a twist of humor to his mouth. "I wasn't exactly naked." Nevertheless, he put on the shirt, not bothering to button it. He swirled the brandy in his glass for a couple of reflective moments, and then he looked up, meeting Elly's wary gaze. "Sit down, honey. I can see I've got some explaining to do."

She looked away. "You've made it clear it's none of my business."

"Yeah, well, knowing it's none of your business doesn't seem to have satisfied you. So sit down, Elly. I'll give you the whole, sordid tale."

"I don't know if I want to hear—"

"Sit down, damn it!"

Elly's mouth tightened resentfully, but she surrendered to the inevitable and took a seat. Jess sighed and walked over to stand in front of the fireplace. Bracing himself against the mantle with one fist, he took another swallow of brandy and began talking in a low, curiously detached tone of voice. Elly had never heard him sound so distant.

"I met Marina Carrington a few years ago. I was thirty-two at the time and had the world in the palm of my hand. I had proven to myself that I was going to be a success in business, and I knew that I was going to be a hell of a lot more successful before I reached forty. I hadn't figured out at that point that I didn't really want to be on the fast track for the rest of my life. That realization came much later. At the time I looked around and thought it all looked pretty damned good. The sky seemed to be the limit. But something was missing.''

Elly slanted him a derisive glance. "The love of a good woman?''

Jess shook his head. "Nothing that simple."

"Simple!"

He ignored the outburst. "When Marina swept into my life I knew right away what I'd been missing. Excitement. In capital letters. It's very seductive at first, maybe even addictive.''

"Excitement?''

"That shot of adrenaline only a creature like Marina can give you. It's sexual and it's very exhilarating. A man never knows what's going to happen next, but he knows it's going to be wild. He feels as if he's standing with one foot on the planet and one about to step off into outer space. When I was thirty-three it was pretty heady stuff. Completely outside my normal realm of experience. You've got to understand, Elly. I had gotten where I was by a lot of hard work, ambition and self-control. Marina came along and turned everything upside down.''

Elly looked down at her clasped hands. "I see.''

Jess glanced at her, frowning. "I'm trying to explain something, Elly. Something that's hard to put into words. Marina was the kind of woman who, when she walked into a room, immediately had the attention of everyone there. She generated some kind of elemental excitement.''

"Lots of feminine charisma, I gather," Elly said evenly.

Jess nodded. "Charisma is probably the word for it. Whatever it is, it seemed to run in the Carrington family."

"It did?"

"Marina had a twin brother. Women react to him the way men react to Marina. Same blond hair and green eyes, the same sense of being bigger than life, not quite real somehow. And both Marina and Damon knew how to exploit their assets. They manipulated everyone around them, and they did it so easily that most people never even realized what had hit them until it was too late."

"A witch and a warlock," Elly whispered, staring into the flames.

Jess glanced at her again, rather sharply. "That's exactly how I came to think of them," he admitted.

"Go on," Elly said with a sense of doom.

"Well, Marina exploded into my life one evening when I was introduced to her at a party. She was very beautiful, very chic and very successful in her own right. She held an executive position in a corporation. I found out later she hadn't climbed up through the ranks purely on merit. Marina used her body to get what she wanted. I knew the minute I looked at her that I wanted her. She knew it, too. And Damon... Damon was always there in the background, watching and laughing, dancing his own circles around women while Marina enthralled the men." Jess broke off, gray eyes filled with dangerous memories. "At any rate, I took her home that night. I couldn't believe my luck when she let me stay until morning. I had set out to seduce her, but looking back on it, I know it was she who seduced me. Like everyone else around her, I let myself be manipulated. In the beginning I was happy enough to participate in my own downfall. Being seen with her was an ego trip for any man. And I enjoyed the trip for a while.''

"It sounds like you were getting what you wanted out of the arrangement,'' Elly said bleakly. "That's not exactly manipulation.''

"You don't understand. No one could understand unless they met Marina or Damon. Never mind. That night was the beginning of an affair that kept me strung out for weeks. At times I thought I was going crazy. She knew how to tease and torment and then satisfy a man. And she knew the secret of repeating the cycle over and over again. She would make me wildly jealous, and then she would laugh at me until I lost control. The battles always ended in bed. She was...very skilled in bed. I thought that if I could put a ring on her finger I could possess her completely.''

Elly wrinkled her nose and sighed. "Did you?''

"Of course not. Things only got worse. Now she was my wife, and in addition to tormenting me with jealousy, she began going through my money at an incredible rate. Such a rate, in fact, that I finally began to get suspicious.''

"Of what?''

"That she was giving the money to another man. It turned out she was. She was giving it to her brother. Damon was plunging into one crazy business scheme after another, using my money as capital. Before I knew it, I found myself bailing him out time after time. As long as he was 'family' I felt obliged to go to his rescue. The two of them were systematically fleecing me. I could hardly believe it, at first. Me, the guy who had been so fast on his feet in the corporate world, who could outmaneuver the best business brains around and who was a natural on the corporate battleground, was getting ripped off by a couple of slick hustlers who never even went to business school!''

"I gather that when you finally realized how much money was involved you came to your senses?" Elly knew the sarcasm simmered in her voice, but she made no real effort to quench it. She was feeling too much pain to worry about good manners.

Jess's expression darkened. He took another long swallow of brandy. "It wasn't just the money. By the time I discovered what was happening on that front I had also begun to realize that I was growing sick of Marina's brand of thrills. The excitement she could generate began to wear. thin. And I was disgusted with myself for letting her put me through the wringer. I was getting plain tired of the aftereffects of her bizarre life-style. Marina, herself, finally realized I wasn't reacting to the old cycle of blazing jealousy followed by blazing sex. When I cut off the endless supply of cash, she opted to head for greener pastures. As it happened, I was already filing for divorce."

"Sounds like the parting of the ways was a mutual decision. How modern."

The line of Jess's jaw seemed to tighten but he didn't respond to her sarcasm. "She left my life the way she had entered it: On the arm of another man. I was incredibly relieved to see her go. I was just as relieved to be rid of her twin. In a strange way, I guess I owe them both something, though."

Elly looked up, eyes widening with further anguish. "What do you owe them?"

Jess's mouth twisted wryly. "It was during the aftermath, when my life was finally settling back down to normal, that I began to look around and ask just what kind of future I was building for myself. Then I asked myself if it was what I really wanted. I finally took stock of myself and my surroundings and began to restructure my thinking. I took a good hard look at every element of my life and began implementing changes. It was then that I started thinking of easing my way out of the business world and making the transition to another kind of environment."

"That was when you decided that what you were really cut out to do was run a quaint little inn on the coast?"

"That's when the idea began to crystallize, yes. But I also made a lot of other fundamental decisions. I knew I no longer needed or wanted the kind of destructive excitement a man gets from a woman like Marina. Once was enough. I would never allow myself to be manipulated like that again. And, above all, I knew I'd never let myself get so close again to being out of control either physically or emotionally."

"You decided you wanted a placid, serene, controlled sort of existence, is that it?" Elly asked tightly, staring hard at his profile. "An uncomplicated life-style that didn't offer too much annoying excitement."

Jess's eyes narrowed faintly. "Something like that."

"And when you met me you decided I'd be just the kind of placid, serene, unexciting sort of wife to fit into that life-style," Elly concluded.

"Elly, you're twisting my words. You don't understand what I'm trying to say."

"Don't I?" she said, her voice flaring. "I know that for two months you haven't shown much interest in making love to the woman you said you wanted to marry. I know that when I decide to take the chance of finding out if you're ever going to want to make love, the first thing that happens is you start seeing Marina's ghost. You did say she was dead, didn't you?"

"Elly, listen to me, you don't know what you're talking about."

"When did she die?"

Jess made an impatient movement, coming away from the mantle toward her. "I heard she was killed in a boating accident a couple of years ago. Elly, that's not important now. I want you to listen to me. I wasn't seeing ghosts tonight." He sat down beside her on the sofa and tried to pull her into his arms. "I saw someone who looked a little like her. That's all."

"You called to her," Elly reminded him bleakly. She evaded his arms and got to her feet. "You called her name."

"Hell, I was startled. It's always startling to see a face out of the fog peering in through the window. Especially one that looks familiar. Elly, you're making too much out of this. It's not like you to get so upset. I want you to calm down and forget about what happened."

"That's not likely, is it? And how do you know it's not like me to get this upset? Even we serene, placid, unexciting types occasionally have our moments. We may not cause quite the sensation you're accustomed to getting, but we're not totally predictable and comfortable, either."

"Elly, you're losing your temper."

"Damn right." She shoved her trembling fingers into the back pockets of her jeans and stood facing him. Challenge and defiance were written in her stance. "I hate to tell you this, but, while losing my temper is rare, it's not exactly the first time it's happened. Believe it or not, I do have a temper."

"I'm beginning to believe it." Slowly Jess got to his feet, his eyes softening as he studied her rigid stance.

"But I'm afraid you're not going to be able to terrorize me with it."

"Why not? Because you've been terrorized by much more exciting displays of temper? You're immune to my more mundane explosions?"

Jess reached out and tugged her gently but forcefully against him, his arms locking around her with undeniable strength. Helpless, Elly stood stiffly, aware of her captor's lips in her tangled hair.

"You aren't going to be able to drive me away from you with a show of temper, honey. I know you too well. Believe me, after my experience with the Carringtons, I became an excellent judge of human nature, my own as well as others. I know you're exactly the kind of woman I want and need. When you've calmed down you'll realize that I'll be a good husband for you."

"If you really think I'd marry you after what happened tonight...!"

Very gently Jess shut off the flow of hot words by putting his fingers against her mouth. He shook his head warningly. "Don't say things you'll only regret in the morning. Trust me, honey. I know what I'm doing, and I know what's best for both of us. We're going to have a good marriage."

"Even if it is a little on the dull side?"

His patience gave a little under the taunting. Jess removed his fingers from her mouth and kissed her, a quick, hard, possessive caress that was unlike any other she'd ever had from him. It was definitely not of the more familiar, more casual variety she had become so well acquainted with during the past two months.

"I don't think we're going to have to worry about boring each other, do you?" he asked with suspicious blandness as he watched the color flood her cheeks. Then he relented, pushing her face gently down onto his shoulder. "Stop worrying, Elly. Everything's going to be fine. You know you want to marry me. You know that you're going to say yes."

"No, I do not know that. And you can give up any idea that I'm going to be pushed into making a decision this weekend. I want more time, Jess. A lot more time. I have a great deal more to consider now. It seems there's a lot I don't know about you."

"That's not true, Elly. You know the real me."

She lifted her head, her eyes overly bright from the effects of unshed tears. "Do I? What happens if you get a sudden craving for the old style of excitement? What if you start seeing Marina's ghost in our bedroom? I'm not sure I can cope with that, Jess."

His face hardened. "Stop it, Elly. You're being ridiculous."

She moved away from him, and he let her go. "You may be right. It's been a traumatic night. Unlike you, I'm not accustomed to so much excitement. I think I'll go to bed."

"Elly—"

"You can have the sofa. There are some sheets and blankets in the hall closet. Help yourself." Without waiting for him to respond, she turned and headed toward the staircase. Her foot was on the first tread when he caught up with her.

"Elly, you're upset and you're overreacting. You need reassurance."

"No kidding." She didn't look at him.

He hesitated and then said deliberately. "I don't think you should spend the night alone."

Her eyes swung to his. Then, half in shock and half in sudden fury, she said, "Are you by any chance offering to reassure me in bed?"

"Why not? After all, what's really changed, Elly? Earlier this evening you made it clear you needed exactly that kind of reassurance. You were begging me for it, in fact. I'm willing to give it to you. By morning you'll know that everything's going to be all right."

Elly was beginning to seethe. "Your generosity overwhelms me. As I said, I just don't think I can handle all this excitement. Good night, Jess. Let me know if you see any more familiar prowlers."

She flung herself up the stairs and into her bedroom. There she closed and locked the door behind her. Then, trembling so violently she was afraid she'd lose her balance, she collapsed onto the bed.

Three

It was the ringing of the telephone that brought Elly out of a fitful sleep the next morning. She struggled awake, vaguely aware that she had forgotten to unplug the instrument downstairs and bring it up to her bedroom before going to bed. Now it was screeching demandingly from the living room and would probably continue to do so until she got downstairs. Then it would undoubtedly stop ringing just as she reached for it.

To her disgusted surprise it ceased clamoring ahead of schedule. She had barely gotten her robe out of the closet when the ringing stopped. Belatedly she realized that Jess must have answered it. She opened her door in time to hear him firmly tell the caller that she was still asleep.

"It's all right, Jess," she said from the top of the stairs. "I'll take it." Hastily fastening her comfortable, warm red flannel robe, she traipsed barefooted down the stairs. Even her robe suited the image Jess had of her, she thought unhappily. Not particularly sexy or exciting, but reliable and comfortable. The mass of tangled chestnut hair hanging around her shoulders probably went with the image, too. She should have taken the time to put on her fluffy bunny slippers. That would have really completed the look.

Jess stood holding the phone, his expression intent as she came down the stairs. He was already dressed, and she wondered just how late it was. Or perhaps he was simply in a hurry to get out of her house. A glance out the window showed that the fog had cleared. Elly let her eyes slide away from his as she took the receiver from him.

"Hello?" When the caller identified herself, the small element of interest Elly had managed to summon up disappeared from her voice. "Oh, it's you, Aunt Clara."

"Elly, dear, I'm calling to tell you that the family has made its decision." Her aunt's aloof, rather arrogant tones held all the certainty in the world.

"I see." Elly slanted a quick glance at Jess, who was listening unabashedly. "And what is the decision?" As if she couldn't guess. She had known from the beginning how the rest of the family intended to vote. She had also known the kind of pressure she would be under once the decision had been made. "And what did you decide, Aunt Clara?"

"We have decided to sell Trentco Switches. I just wanted to let you know so that you would be prepared to vote at the meeting. I think it is essential that we present a united front. You know Harrigan will fight us."

Good for Harrigan, Elly thought. But she kept her voice carefully polite as she said, "Thank you for telling me your decision, Aunt Clara. I will certainly take it into consideration."

"Come now, Elly, you know there's no need to consider the matter." Aunt Clara's tone was suddenly sharp. "We have let you know what we intend to do, and it will be best for all concerned if you refrain from causing trouble. You have absolutely no knowledge of this sort of thing. What could you possibly know about buyouts and mcrgcr offers? Oh, maybe once upon a time you could have dealt with these matters, but not any longer. The business world has passed you by, and you should have sense enough to know it. Living out there with that bunch of ex-hippies, the way you do, it's a wonder you're not on food stamps and welfare. I feel so sorry for your parents. I can't imagine what they must think these days. And if it had been your mother calling this morning she would have been shocked to the core."

Elly bristled. "Why would my mother have been shocked, Aunt Clara?"

"Don't play games with me, Elly. You know perfectly well I'm talking about the fact that a strange man answered your phone this morning. I have to assume that's a regular occurrence these days. Only to be expected considering the sort of life-style you're leading. If I were you, I would at least instruct your male friends not to answer the telephone at seven forty-five in the morning. It gives a very bad impression. But, of course, I suppose that's your business."

Elly's fingers tightened around the receiver. "Yes, Aunt Clara. Considering the fact that I'm thirty years old and self-supporting, I'd say it definitely is my business. Now, if you don't mind, I haven't even had coffee yet, and I'm due to open the store in an hour. I appreciate you informing me of your decision. As I said, I will take it under advisement. Goodbye, Aunt Clara."

She hung up the phone before her aunt had finished sputtering in her ear. "This is not starting out to be one of my more scintillating days. Did you know you give a very bad impression on the phone, Jess?"

"I'll have to work on my telephone manners." He spoke offhandedly as he watched her face. "That rather rude woman is your aunt?"

"Unfortunately." Elly stalked toward the kitchen. "Any coffee?"

"Not yet. I just came in from outside. Haven't had time to make it." He followed her to the kitchen door, his eyes never leaving her as she busied herself with the coffee pot.

"What were you doing outside? Are you a jogging freak or something?" Elly asked irritably as she ran water into the pot. The way he was watching her made her more aware than ever of her rumpled, unexciting appearance. None of the fantasies she had ever had about her first morning with Jess Winter had gone quite like this.

"No. I just wanted to have a look around to see if I could find any trace of last night's visitor."

Elly's head came up quickly. "And did you?"

"Afraid not. It rained around four in the morning. Whatever evidence there might have been was long gone by the time I got outside. Don't look at me like that, Elly," he added too mildly. "There really *was* someone out there."

"I'm not going to argue the point. Lord knows I've got enough of an argument on my hands as it is."

"Something to do with your Aunt Clara?" Jess dropped casually into a seat by the window.

"Aunt Clara and most of my other relatives except my parents who are, thank goodness, out of the country."

"What's the problem?"

Elly sighed. "It's a long story. I'm sure you've got better things to do."

"Nope. Not a thing. Tell me the story, Elly."

"Look, Jess, I have to be at work in an hour. I don't have time for a long chat. Do you mind?" She hovered grimly over the coffee machine, waiting impatiently for it to brew.

"You can talk and make breakfast at the same time."

"Good grief. You're as bad as Aunt Clara. Why is everyone in my life so damned arrogant?"

"I don't think of myself as being arrogant. I think of it as being assertive."

She caught the thread of amusement in the words and glanced up sharply. Jess smiled benignly.

"Maybe I should take notes on assertiveness. It certainly seems to work for the rest of you," Elly grumbled. She poured coffee and began rummaging around in a cupboard for some granola cereal.

"Oh? Is it going to work for your aunt, then? Going to give her whatever it is she wants?"

"Not if I can help it. If she thinks I'm going to sell off the family inheritance, she's out of her mind," Elly said, flashing a determined look.

"What puts you in the position of even being able to sell off a family inheritance?"

Elly groaned. "You never give up, do you? You just keep pushing and prodding until you have an answer." She carried the canister of cereal and a carton of milk over to the table and they both sat down.

"I told you: assertiveness."

It was Elly who gave up. "I'll give you a short summary of the situation. My father's brother, Uncle Toby, founded a company called Trentco. When he died he left a sizable block of shares to me—controlling interest, in fact. Not that I wanted them, mind you, but because good old Uncle Toby knew his own relatives. He had a pretty fair hunch they'd sell off the company if they got the chance. Having put his life's blood into the firm, my uncle wanted to see it kept intact for the next generation of Trents. He had hopes someone like me or possibly my cousin Dave, or even one of the younger kids, might take charge of the firm someday. Now the rest of the family has decided they want to sell Trentco. We've had a good offer, and they've all had delusions of instant wealth.''

"So the rest of the family is putting pressure on you to vote the controlling block of shares in favor of the sale?''

"No wonder you were so good in business. You're so fast on your feet.''

Jess grinned. "You are grouchy in the mornings, aren't you? What does Trentco make?''

"Widgits.''

He arched one heavy eyebrow. "Widgits?''

"You know, little things like switches and wiring and stuff.''

"Oh. Widgits.''

"Yes. And I'm not going to vote to sell the company because my cousin Dave has shown a serious interest in it. He wants to keep it. He's studying business, and he seems to have an aptitude for that. In a few more years he'll be able to handle it. He has every right to his inheritance. And I've got a couple of little nieces whose mother needs the steady income, although she doesn't always think far enough ahead to realize it. She's too interested in the prospect of quick money.''

"So to protect the inheritance all you have to do is hold firm against Aunt Clara and the crowd?''

"Who all think I'm the typical product of an overly liberal education: An impractical, nonconforming, left-wing dropout of uncertain morals—except that after this morning, Aunt Clara is no longer uncertain about my morals."

"Because I answered the phone?"

"Yeah."

"You should have told her that you were going to marry me."

"But I don't know that I am going to marry you," Elly retorted very carefully.

"Sure you are." He leaned across the table and covered her hand. "Nothing has changed. All you have to do is admit that to yourself. Then everything can return to normal."

"It's because things weren't exactly normal between us that I started getting nervous in the first place!"

"Hence the big seduction scene last night?"

She flushed, concentrating on her granola. "I'm sure it must have been quite tame as seduction scenes go—I mean, considering what you're accustomed to in that line."

Jess didn't move, but the change in him was immediate and unmistakable. Elly shifted uneasily, knowing she had gone too far. Involuntarily she looked up to find him staring at her with the depths of winter in his eyes.

"Believe it or not, your style of seduction was a totally new experience for me. I've never had a woman ask me so sweetly or so honestly to make love to her. I'm used to games in that line, Elly. Not the real thing. I find I like the real thing very much. I'd like another chance."

Elly lurched to her feet and dropped her dishes into the sink. "I've got to get ready for work, Jess. It's getting late, and you know I have to open the shop at nine. Excuse me while I get dressed. Perhaps I'll, uh, see you later or something," she ended lamely as she hurried toward the door.

"You know damn well you're going to see me later, Elly," he said behind her, but she was already halfway to the stairs.

Some of the old anger and frustration came back as Jess watched Elly vanish. He owed this mess to Marina. Was the woman going to haunt him in one way or another for the rest of his life? Coldly, Jess dampened the threatening waves of fury. Marina was gone. He would not allow her to interfere in his new relationship with Elly.

Elly was a gentle, reasonable woman. She would calm down and return to her normal, even-tempered self. She just needed a little time. She wouldn't, she *couldn't* continue to hold the past against him.

But Jess knew deep down that matters would have been different this morning if Elly's sweet seduction scene last night had been allowed to continue to its conclusion. Everything would have been so much simpler today. Elly would have had the reassurance she needed that she was wanted and he... Jess paused, contemplating fully just what it was he had let slip away. He would have had a kind of warmth and closeness he'd never known. And he would have had one more bond between himself and Elly.

Jess swore softly and got to his feet to continue clearing the table. He had been a fool to waste so much time. He should have been making love to Elly for nearly two months. It seemed an act of malicious fate that, when at last matters in that department were finally going to get sorted out, something interfered.

Not something. Someone. Someone who looked a hell of a lot like Marina Carrington. Jess paused by the sink, thinking that last thought through. The only person he knew who looked a lot like Marina was her twin, Damon.

By the middle of the afternoon Elly had finally begun to come to terms with her reaction to the news of Jess's past. She had spent most of the day rationalizing, lecturing, analyzing and assessing. Jess had had the sensitivity to stay away from the shop. She assumed he was busy talking to the local contractors and craftsmen he would need to start the renovation work on the charming Victorian fantasy he intended to turn into a quiet, luxury inn. Uncertain as to what he would do at the end of the day, Elly busied herself stocking shelves and waiting on customers and tried not to think about the evening ahead.

The Natural Choice was one of those small-town community stores that become a meeting place for people who live nearby. In addition to buying the flours, grains, tofu and other assorted grocery products Elly stocked, local people dropped in to chat, catch up on news or just hang out. Everyone knew everybody else and shared information freely. It would have been impossible for the proprietor of such a shop to keep a romance quiet, and Elly had made no effort to do so. Everyone in the community knew of Jess Winter and his plans for the old mansion. They also knew Elly had been dating him steadily for two months. So Elly was prepared for casual inquiries even though she could cheerfully have done without them today.

"How's your friend, Elly? Thought I saw him over at Wilson's this morning?" Sarah Mitchell hoisted a gurgling eighteen-month-old baby onto her hip and reached into her handcrafted leather purse for her wallet. Everything about Sarah was handcrafted—from the long, paisley cotton skirt she had designed herself, to the fringed leather vest she wore over a denim shirt. Her hair reached to her waist and fell in a long heavy braid down her back. The baby, who went by the name of Compass Rose and who wasn't yet old enough to mind the unusual appelation, was dressed in a handknitted jumpsuit.

"I think he said something about wanting Wilson to do some woodwork in the hall," Elly murmured, packing rye flour, whole wheat pasta and tofu into a paper sack. She didn't particularly want to discuss Jess today, but she knew the questions were unavoidable. In the two months he had been coming and going between Portland and the coast, Jess had managed to make himself a familiar and welcome presence in town.

"Is he still going to want the stained-glass work?" Sarah asked a little uncertainly.

Elly suddenly realized what was making her customer anxious. She smiled reassuringly. "Don't worry, Sarah. He won't change his mind about the stained-glass order he mentioned to you. Once he makes a commitment like that he follows through."

Sarah nodded, looking relieved. "Good. The truth is, I could use the work."

"No check this month?" Elly asked commiseratingly.

The other woman shook her head. "No, and I think I'd better get used to the fact that there aren't going to be any more checks. Mark is long gone, Elly. He's not coming back. I've accepted that now, but it means I can't treat the stained glass as a hobby any longer. I've got to start making it pay. Or else I've got to find another kind of job."

"Jess will pay well for the beautiful work you do, Sarah. Don't worry," Elly said gently. Then, unobtrusively, she added several more ounces of whole-wheat pasta to the order. What the heck. Pasta was relatively cheap and the whole wheat was nutritious for little Compass Rose. Elly figured she wouldn't miss the profit on the few ounces of pasta. Sarah Mitchell could certainly use the extra food. Elly thought bleakly about the kind of man who would get a woman pregnant and then leave to "find himself." Jess Winter would never do that. Never in a million years.

"Your Jess is a good man, Elly."

"Yes." The kind of man who would follow through on his commitment to buy stained glass from an artist who was having trouble making ends meet. The kind of man who would not get a woman pregnant and then abandon her. Yes, Elly thought, Jess was a good man. His fundamental integrity was one of the things that had made her fall in love with him. She just wished he was in love with her the way she was with him—wildly, passionately, head-over-heels in love.

"Well, tell him I'm available whenever he's ready to have me start designing. I'll—" Sarah broke off as the bell over the door chimed cheerfully. "I'll . . . good heavens," she went on in a low tone. "Where did he come from?"

"Who? Jess? Is he here?" Suddenly tense, Elly turned to glance at whoever had opened the door and found herself blinking in astonishment at the newcomer. Sarah was still staring herself. And no wonder, Elly thought in a rush of amusement. It wasn't every day a man like this walked into The Natural Choice. "Looks like something from a calendar of 'hunks,'" she murmured.

The man who stood in the doorway nodded easily, apparently taking the feminine stares as his due. He strode forward with a nonchalance that told its own tale. This man was accustomed to being the center of attention. He was, without a doubt, the handsomest male Elly had ever seen. Tall, lean, with curly blond hair and perfectly chiseled features, he had a casual, sexy, inviting smile and a promise of excitement in his green eyes.

Green eyes, Elly thought suddenly. But there was no time to dwell on the bizarre notion that had just struck her. The man had reached the counter and with unerring instinct was already making the one move calculated to put everyone at ease. He was focusing the full force of his attention, something a few women Elly had met would have killed for, on Compass Rose.

"Hey, beautiful," he murmured to the wide-eyed toddler. "Where have you been all my life?"

"Her name is Compass Rose," Sarah explained hastily, bemused by the attention the handsome man was paying to her child.

"Compass Rose," the stranger repeated in a soft drawl. "Something tells me she's going to lead a lot of men astray during the next few years." He lifted a finger and chucked the baby under her chin.

Compass Rose's eyes got even wider and then, without warning, she started wailing. Turning her face into her mother's denim shirt, she clung fiercely, her high-pitched cry filling the shop.

"What in the world?" Startled, Sarah cradled the child closer. She cast an apologetic look at the newcomer. "I'm sorry. She's usually very good with strangers. I don't know what could have gotten into her. I guess I better get her out of here. Thanks, Elly. I'll see you later this week. You won't forget to remind Jess that I'm ready any time he is, will you?"

"I won't forget," Elly mouthed above the wails of Compass Rose. Sarah fled from the shop, cuddling the baby.

"Well," the stranger said philosophically as the door closed on the child's cries, "I guess I'm not that good with the younger set." He leaned on the counter and smiled at Sarah. "But I'm hell on wheels with older women."

Elly blinked owlishly and wondered why she felt the irrational desire to do the same as Compass Rose had done and start screaming. "Perhaps you'd like to meet my Aunt Clara," she said instead. "She's in her sixties so I guess she'd qualify as an older woman."

Green eyes flashed wickedly. "I had in mind something midrange."

Elly summoned up a polite, shopkeeper's smile. "Did you? Well, I'm sure you'll find it. Let me know if you need any assistance while shopping. There are some handbaskets over by the bread counter and one old shopping cart that I keep for emergencies. I'm afraid this isn't exactly a supermarket."

"I'm only looking for one particular item." He didn't move from the counter.

"Just as well, I'll be closing soon, anyway. What was it you wanted?"

"I came here to meet someone."

"I'm afraid I don't—"

"Nothing to be concerned about," the stranger said easily. "I've got lots of time. Some things are better if they aren't rushed." Then he reached out, the same way he had to Compass Rose and caught Elly lightly under her chin.

She was so startled by the audacity of the man that it took Elly a few seconds to realize what he was doing. Then, before she could react to the overfamiliar touch, the shop bell chimed again as the door opened. Without even looking in that direction Elly knew who stood on the threshold.

Far too gently, Jess closed the door behind himself and stood taking in the sight of Elly's uncertain, wary expression as the other man's hand dropped from her chin. Then, as if there was no particular importance about the matter, he glanced at the blond-haired, green-eyed newcomer.

Elly's pulse was racing as if she'd found herself in a fight-or-flight situation rather than safely behind the counter of her shop. She watched Jess walk calmly down the aisle to where she stood behind the waist-high barrier. The room seemed to be filled with strange tension. A part of her urged flight, but another element warned that there was no safe place to run. Then Jess was flattening his palms on the polished counter, leaning across it to kiss her with seeming casualness.

Elly didn't resist, but she knew her lips must have been as cold as his. This was not a kiss of warmth or even casual affection. This was a public announcement for the benefit of the green-eyed man who stood watching in amusement. Coolly, Jess straightened and turned to confront the other man.

"Well, Carrington, I would have been happy to live the rest of my life without ever seeing you again. But I guess that was too much to hope for. What the hell brings you here?"

Damon Carrington smiled, and Elly cringed inwardly.

"Is that any way to greet family?" Damon asked mildly.

"You're not family. Not anymore." Jess leaned against the counter, his pose deceptively cool. "I'm not overflowing with patience this afternoon. What do you want?"

"What makes you so sure I'm after something?"

"It's your nature."

Damon considered that. "Maybe you're right."

"So what is it this time?"

"Going to give me what I want without a fight, Winter? That's not like you. I expected to have to work at this a little." Damon glanced at Elly's still face. "But maybe you've got other things to worry about these days, hmm? Little projects you wouldn't want jeopardized. She's not too bad, Jess. Not in Marina's league, of course, but how many women are?" He started to lift his hand again, apparently planning to recapture Elly's chin. Green eyes examined her with calculating interest.

Jess didn't move. "Touch her and I'll kill you, Carrington."

The threat hovered in the air, as real as the man who had made it. Damon's eyes narrowed in amusement, but he dropped his hand. "Well, well. This is serious, isn't it?"

"I think it's time for you to leave, Carrington. Elly is going to close the shop, aren't you, Elly?" He pinned her with his glance. The command radiated from him in waves.

Elly didn't even make a pretense of resisting. She wanted out of that tension-fraught room more than anyone could have imagined. "Yes," she said firmly, "I am." Quickly she began readying the cash register.

"No need to run, Winter. I can find you easily enough. It's a small town, isn't it? A little too small for you, I would have said."

"Small towns have their advantages. It's easy to keep track of unwanted strangers. You might keep that in mind."

Damon shook his head sadly. "You surprise me, Winter. I would have expected you to keep going in the fast lane. All the way to the top, wherever that is. People used to say the sky was the limit where you were concerned. Now look at you, getting ready to run an inn in a sleepy little village on the coast. Picked just the right kind of woman to go with your new life-style, didn't you? She looks sweet, Winter. Maybe a little too sweet for you. After all, you're accustomed to something with a little more tang, aren't you? I never—Hey! Damn you, what the hell do you think . . . ?"

"Jess!" Elly whirled around, stunned to see Jess come away from the counter in a smooth, coiled movement.

He had Damon flattened against the wall before Elly fully realized what had happened. Raw menace etched Jess's face, and his eyes were like ice as he leaned forward. His voice was a harsh whisper.

"Get out of here, Carrington. Don't let me see you again. Is that very clear? I swear as God is my witness I won't be able to guarantee your safety if I ever see you again. If you come near Elly I can promise you that I'll make you pay."

Damon hissed, "Pay? You're the one who's going to pay, Winter. You owe me!"

"For what?"

"For what you did to Marina!"

"I didn't do a damn thing to her except divorce her. And as I recall she was already tired of me anyway. Are you crazy, Carrington?"

"She's dead!"

"I didn't kill her and you damn well know it," Jess growled.

"She'd be alive today if it hadn't been for you."

"What the hell are you talking about?"

"You cut her off without a penny," Damon said accusingly.

"So? She'd socked away plenty while she was married to me. Not exactly my fault if she didn't invest it! You *are* crazy."

"She wouldn't have had to sleep with that old bastard if it hadn't been for the way you left her high and dry."

"I get it," Jess said wearily. "If she hadn't been sleeping with him for his money she wouldn't have been on his yacht when it capsized. Therefore, it's all my fault. Is that your logic? You're out of your mind, Carrington." He released his victim. "Get away from me. I don't want to see you anywhere near Elly again. *Get out of here!*"

Damon moved warily away from the wall, straightening his rumpled black shirt. "You owe me, Winter."

Jess ignored him, reaching for Elly's arm as she came around the counter. "Are you ready?"

"Yes," she whispered, shaken by the violence. "Yes, I'm ready."

The chime sounded as the door closed abruptly behind Damon Carrington. Elly jumped a little at the noise. "Excitement," she said almost inaudibly.

"What?" Jess was turning off the lights with swift, chopping motions of his hand.

"You said the Carringtons brought excitement into one's life. I don't think I'm into excitement, Jess. Not if that's any sample of it."

Jess halted at the door, turning to look down at her. His eyes were fierce. "And you're not going to get 'into' it. You're not going to get anywhere near it, do you understand? I don't want you in the same room with Damon Carrington. Elly, I've seen Carrington in action.

The man's a warlock where women are concerned. He casts spells on them.''

"Not on all women," she denied.

"You don't know what I'm talking about."

"Little Compass Rose hated him on sight." *And it didn't take me much longer to hate him,* Elly added silently. She had begun to hate and fear Damon Carrington the moment she realized he was a threat to Jess.

"Compass Rose? Oh, you mean Sarah Mitchell's kid. I'm not talking about his effect on children. But I've seen him manipulate women, and they're like putty in his hands. Stay out of his way. Do you understand me, Elly?"

"I understand." She couldn't think of anything else to say. Her instinct was to give him the agreement he demanded and then change the subject. Once again she found herself hesitating to push Jess.

Out on the street there was no sign of Carrington. Elly was grateful. "Sarah said to tell you that she could do the stained-glass designs whenever you were ready. The sooner the better, Jess."

It was obvious Jess still had other things on his mind. He frowned down at Elly. "Why sooner? I've got that work scheduled a couple of months downstream."

"There's been no word from Mark. No money either."

Jess nodded abruptly. "I get it. The bastard's skipped, huh? Okay, I'll talk to her tomorrow. I'll give her an advance on the job. That should hold her for a while."

"Thank you, Jess." A good man, Elly thought.

"Elly?"

"Yes?"

"I meant what I said a minute ago. Stay away from Carrington. He's poison."

It occurred to Elly that she had never seen Jess Winter so passionate about anything before, except for those brief moments last night when he had finally begun to make love to her. "It's obvious the Carringtons, brother and sister, had a fairly traumatic effect on you, Jess."

"It's trauma I can do without repeating. Remember how you once told me that you loved to live near the ocean, that you like looking at it, watching the changing weather on it, walking alongside it, but that you never ever went swimming in it?"

"I remember." It was the truth. She never swam in the sea.

"Well, treat Damon Carrington the same way."

"Look, but don't touch?"

"I don't even want you looking at him."

She smiled tremulously and not without a touch of hope. "Are you telling me that you might be capable of feeling a little jealousy over me?"

The ill-advised remark stopped him in his tracks. "Lady, you don't know what you're talking about. You haven't got the least idea of what jealousy does to people, so don't try to tease me. I want your word of honor that you'll steer clear of Carrington."

"Oh, Jess, I never meant . . ."

"Your word, Elly," he repeated roughly, his fingers sinking almost painfully into her shoulders.

She looked up at him with gentle assurance. "Jess, you don't have to worry about Carrington putting a spell on me. I feel toward him very much the way Compass Rose does."

He watched her for a moment and then seemed to come to some inner conclusion. "Good. Keep it that way."

She would, Elly thought with a sense of resignation, because she loved Jess too much ever to let herself be used against him, even if it was only his pride that was at stake. But she couldn't help wishing that more than his pride and self-respect were involved.

A part of her wished Jess loved her so passionately that he might truly be vulnerable to the fear of losing her to another man. As it was, she was very much aware that his reactions to Carrington stemmed from the unpleasantness of the past and from an angry pride that refused to let a woman lead him through hell again.

Four

On Monday morning Elly gave in to the impulse to take a walk on the beach before opening The Natural Choice. She'd taken Sunday off as usual, but the day had not been a particularly relaxing one. This morning she was tense and restless.

Jess had left for Portland the previous evening. At least he'd stopped pressuring her for an answer to his proposal, Elly thought unhappily. He finally seemed to sense that she needed more time to come to terms with the situation. She had known instinctively that he hadn't wanted to give her that additional time, and in a way it surprised her. Until now Jess had acted as if there was no rush about anything in life. He had been content to let matters take their course. But, then, that was probably because until now Jess had set the course himself. The schedule might have seemed loose, Elly decided, but it had been in place. Subtly, calmly, quietly, Jess Winter had been in control of events all along.

Until the past had intruded.

There had been no sign of Damon Carrington since Saturday afternoon. No one in town seemed to have seen him and that apparently reassured Jess. Elly had a hunch that if there had been any indication that Carrington was still around, Jess would have found an excuse not to return to Portland. It would have been an expensive excuse because these last few weeks in the city were important from a business standpoint. Jess was winding up a lucrative consulting assignment and finalizing his financial arrangements for the forthcoming change in his life-style. It would have constituted another unwelcome change in his plans.

The tide was out this morning, and Elly took pleasure in exploring the nooks and crannies that were underwater at other times. The beach here was a rocky one, with a number of fascinating tidepools, encrusted formations and miniature worlds tucked away in the rocks. The small cove was dominated by a huge boulder that crouched aloofly in the center. When the tide was in, there was no way to reach it. Foaming water surged around it, acting like a moat around a castle. But this morning it stood undefended, prepared to yield its secrets to anyone who was willing to cross the damp, packed sand.

Elly had explored the rock castle before, but it never ceased to interest her. Starfish clung to its base, small fish swam in pools of trapped water and a variety of crustaceans scampered over the surface in an endless quest for food.

The sea was an alien world to Elly, one she found enthralling but also one she feared on some levels. It was all very well to study its creatures while they were exposed and vulnerable. The thought of meeting them in their natural environment while the tide was in struck a primitive chord of genuine fear. And it wasn't just the life forms of the sea she feared. The power of the surging waves was equally disturbing. Elly could swim, but she never swam in the sea. She hadn't since that one terrifying afternoon on a southern California beach.

But this morning she poked around the huge boulder in the quiet cove with her usual interest, her mind occupied with the problem of Jess Winter.

She had been belatedly astonished by her initial reaction to the threat of Damon Carrington. Her instincts had been to defend Jess, but that was ridiculous. If anyone could take care of himself, it was Jess Winter. Perhaps a woman always felt that way about the man she loved.

"Ah, Jess," she muttered, turning away from the exposed boulder to start back toward the house, "do you think you'll ever let yourself really fall in love again?" And if he did, was she the kind of woman he would choose?

Comfortable, even-tempered, sweet. Elly ran through the irritating list of adjectives Jess so often applied to her, and she wanted to scream. The list hardly allowed for passion and love. But, then, Jess didn't want to allow for either of those potentially dangerous emotions in his life.

Elly thought of those brief moments Friday night when at last she had stirred real desire in him. It was foolish to cling to such thoughts and try to build on them. After all, it was perfectly possible for a man to have his sexual appetite aroused without having any real love aroused with it.

In any event, the whole project had foundered because of a face at the window. Not for the first time, Elly wondered if it had been Damon Carrington peering into her living room that night. In the dark and the fog would Jess have briefly mistaken Damon for his twin?

Reluctantly Elly climbed the cliff path. At the top she turned one last time to gaze out at the everchanging sea. The chilled early morning breeze whipped at her braids, loosing strands of hair that blew into her eyes. Perhaps it was those tendrils that were causing the threat of tears.

The phone rang that evening just as Elly was sitting down to a quiet meal in the kitchen. The possibility that it might be Aunt Clara almost kept her from answering. The probability that it might be Jess made Elly stretch out her hand.

"Oh, Jess, I'm glad it's you."

"Who were you expecting?" There was an unfamiliar edge to the question.

"I was afraid it might be Aunt Clara."

Jess seemed to relax on the other end of the line. "Has she been pestering you?"

"No, but she will as the time of the stockholders' meeting gets closer," Elly predicted. "Aunt Clara is very persistent, especially where money is concerned."

"I've been thinking about that situation, Elly." Jess suddenly sounded all business. "Why don't I look into it for you? If Aunt Clara and the family knew you had some, er..."

"High-priced firepower to back me, she might stop bothering me?" Elly concluded with a quick grin. "Jess, I couldn't afford even half your usual fee."

"For you I'll work cheap."

"How cheap?"

He paused and then said blandly, "An answer to my proposal would be sufficient. A *yes* answer, that is."

Elly's brief humor faded. "Jess, please don't push."

"Honey, there's no reason to hesitate and you know it." He seemed to want to pursue the argument but instead changed the subject. "Carrington hasn't shown up has he?"

"No."

"Good. I want you to let me know immediately if he does. Understand, Elly?"

"I understand." Elly wondered how Jess could suddenly sound so cold and forbidding. Only a few seconds ago he had been trying to coax her into agreeing to marry him.

"Eating dinner?"

"How did you guess?"

"Just a hunch, based on the fact that I'm about to eat mine. What are you having?"

"Leftover lentil casserole and a glass of that Washington State cabernet wine I had tucked away in the cupboard."

"Sounds good. Better than the frozen dinner I just put into the oven. I'll be down early on Friday, Elly."

Elly's hand clenched in unexpected nervousness. "Fine."

"I think you should be able to have your answer ready by then, don't you?" The question was cool and pointed.

"I—I don't know, Jess."

"I think you do, honey. Stop dragging it out. You know this is what you want. Goodnight, Elly."

"Goodnight, Jess." Unhappily she replaced the receiver. He had cut off the conversation so quickly tonight. Usually Jess talked for half an hour when he called.

The phone rang almost immediately. Elly reached for it without thinking, and this time it was Aunt Clara. With a stifled groan, Elly forced herself to listen politely while her aunt went through a harangue about the financial reasons for selling Trentco. There was no attempt at a discussion; it was purely a lecture.

Elly was exhausted by the time she hung up and for the first time she wondered if things might not be easier if she let Jess represent her. Dealing with family was always an emotionally taxing situation, especially when the relatives in question were Trents. Maybe a disinterested third party could exert a calming, persuasive influence.

The drawback to involving Jess in the thorny family situation was that it meant involving him more deeply in her life at a time when Elly was wondering if it wouldn't be best to end the relationship.

It was Sarah Mitchell who reminded her the next day of the potluck gathering scheduled for Wednesday evening.

"Good Lord, I almost forgot," Elly exclaimed. "I'm supposed to take my world-famous lentil casserole."

"I didn't know you had a famous lentil casserole. Last time you brought a salad, didn't you?"

"Believe me, this sucker is going to be famous after Wednesday evening. I've been working on it for months. I think I've got it tuned to perfection. Jess seems to like it, at any rate. What are you bringing, Sarah?"

"Thanks to the advance I got from Jess I think I can manage my usual whole wheat pasta salad. By the way, I've already started designing some glass for the entryway of his inn. I went out to the place this morning and did some studies. I'm really looking forward to doing the work."

Sarah's enthusiasm was heartwarming. Little Compass Rose jabbered contentedly while the adults talked, and Elly privately concluded that both the child and her mother were probably going to be better off without the unreliable influence of Mark Casey in their lives.

That realization made Elly think of Jess. Whatever qualms she had about marrying him weren't based on any fears of his unreliability. Jess was the kind of man you could count on when the chips were down. Elly knew that with a deep-seated instinct.

The potluck on Wednesday was a casual meeting of neighbors and friends that Elly fully expected to enjoy. A month ago a similar party had been held at the house of a local artisan who lived fairly close to Elly. Tonight, however, a different couple had opened their home, and this time Elly had been obliged to drive several miles to the farmsite. Ann Palmer and her husband, Jim, had recently moved to Oregon from California and were intent on pursuing a back-to-the-land life-style. It remained to be seen whether they would be successful in making the farm produce, but in the meantime they were thoroughly enjoying their new life.

"Elly! There you are. I was wondering where you were." Ann Palmer approached to take the lentil casserole as her guest walked in the door. "Next month we all expect Jess to accompany you to these gala social bashes. He'll have completed his move by then, won't he?"

"If all goes according to schedule," Elly agreed diplomatically. "And where Jess is concerned, nearly everything does go according to schedule." She glanced around the room full of casually dressed craftsmen, artists, small-time farmers and boutique proprietors and wondered whether Jess knew what he would be getting into socially. Probably. He always seemed to know what he was doing.

Half an hour later Elly was in the middle of an intense discussion concerning the merits of growing one's own sprouts when the roomful of people underwent that strange phenomena of going quiet all at once. Instinctively Elly glanced toward the door, and quite suddenly she knew what Jess had meant when he had tried to explain the Carringtons' impact on a crowd.

Damon Carrington stood in the doorway, smiling in secret amusement as everyone glanced at the tall figure. He was dressed all in black and a lock of blond hair curled rakishly over one brow. His green eyes moved over the curious faces with no sign of self-consciousness, just a hint of condescension. He was not alone. At his side was Sarah Mitchell, looking happier than Elly had seen her since Mark had left.

Elly watched her friend in dismay, but she knew immediately there would be no point trying to warn her about Damon. The Carrington charm was clearly at work and highly effective. Little Compass Rose had apparently been left with a sitter for the evening. Elly wondered if the child had been wailing when her mother left with the strange man.

The hum of activity started up again, and Elly excused herself to get some more salad from the long table that had been set up against one wall. As far as she was concerned, her pleasure in the friendly evening had just evaporated. Damon Carrington was still around and that, she knew in her bones, meant trouble.

"Hi, Elly. You met Damon the other day, remember?" Sarah's voice was bubbling with enthusiasm. "I ran into him yesterday again when I went out to Jess's inn to make some more sketches. Wasn't that a coincidence? Damon is very fond of Victorian architecture, aren't you Damon?"

"Fascinated." Damon's brilliant green eyes swept over Elly. She wanted to cringe from that gaze, and found she had to make an effort to act nonchalantly. "I understand you have a very interesting place yourself, Elly."

"Nothing spectacular," she assured him quickly. "Just an old, updated beach cottage, actually."

"I'd like to see it sometime," he murmured.

"I'm afraid I really don't . . ."

Before Elly could finish her horrified excuse, Sarah was interrupting cheerfully. "I told Damon he would probably be bored to tears tonight, but he insisted on coming along. Said he wanted to see what life was like in a small beach town."

"I imagine it's a real change for you, Damon," Elly said coolly.

"I'm highly adaptable."

"I'll just bet you are," Elly murmured. She sipped her hot spiced cider and tried to think of a way to escape from the small confrontation.

"Damon says he'd like to take me and Compass Rose to the beach tomorrow. Wouldn't that be nice?" Sarah reached around Elly to help herself to a small sandwich.

"It's too cold for swimming," Damon said, accepting the sandwich from Sarah with a charming smile, "but I thought Compass Rose might enjoy playing on the beach."

"It's always too cold for swimming as far as Elly is concerned," Sarah said with a laugh. "She hates the water, don't you Elly? She's afraid of sharks and things. Has a real phobia about swimming in the sea."

"I didn't realize there were sharks in these waters," Damon said, eyeing Elly with interest.

"The truth is," Elly said blandly, "most of the sharks are on land. Which is lucky, I guess. So much easier to spot them that way." She didn't wait to see if Damon had gotten the point. Instead she slipped away from the pot-luck table with a smile. "Now, if you'll excuse me I want to talk to Ruth and Liz about that quilt they're doing for me. I'll see you later, Sarah."

"Right," Sarah smiled and turned back to bask in the attention of the handsomest male at the gathering.

From a discrete distance Elly watched her friend during the rest of the evening, knowing there was really nothing she could do to interfere. Damon had set out to make a conquest. It was easy to see, Elly decided, just what a captivating effect Damon Carrington had on women. Every female in the room was aware of him. When they spoke to him they bubbled with enthusiasm; their eyes were a little brighter, the conversation a little more intense. There was a feeling of excitement in the air. Elly could imagine what the impact on the males would be if a female version of Damon had walked into the room. She began to see what Marina Carrington must have been like in action. It was frightening.

By ten o'clock the good-natured crowd began to break up. Sarah left with Damon, her eyes still too excited as far as Elly was concerned. She worried for her friend, but she didn't know what to do. Sarah had been so unhappy for so many months it seemed cruel to step in and try to blight the one spark that had come into her life. You couldn't make other people's decisions for them, Elly told herself as she helped Ann Palmer clean up the old farmhouse parlor.

"Drive carefully, Elly. The fog is starting to get heavy out there. Take it easy going home." Ann smiled as Elly collected the empty casserole dish.

"Don't worry, I'll be careful. It was a lovely evening, Ann."

"That Carrington man certainly livened things up, didn't he? He's almost too good looking somehow. Like something out of a magazine ad."

Elly nodded, glad that at least one other woman in the room had realized that fact. "I agree with you. It's as if he's not quite real. Or quite human."

"I'll stick with my Jim, I think," Ann confided lightly. "One thing you can say for Jim; he's human!" She grinned at her bearded husband, who was scooping up paper plates. Jim growled a laughing response as Ann turned back to Elly. "You'll do fine with your Jess. By the way, that casserole was fantastic. What's the secret?"

"Wine, molasses and ground chili peppers. Took a while to get the proportions down right."

"How many times have you experimented with it on Jess?"

Elly winced, remembering how frequently Jess had found himself eating a different version of lentil casserole during the past two months. "I hate to think about it. He never complained, though."

"He wouldn't. He values homecooking too much. The last time I saw him at the store he told me he couldn't wait to get it full-time."

"Then he should hire a cook!"

Ann Palmer's expression softened. "Elly, believe me, there's nothing wrong in having a man like your cooking. That old cliché about the way to a man's heart being through his stomach didn't get to be a cliché by being untrue, you know. Clichés get to be clichés just because they do contain an element of truth. He's a good man, your Jess."

Elly smiled politely and hastened out to her car. *If only he really were my Jess,* she thought. *Completely, une-*

quivocally, wholeheartedly mine. Damned if she was going to let herself be married for her cooking and other convenient skills!

The interior of the car was cold, and the engine resisted starting. When she finally got it going, Elly sat in the darkness for a few minutes, letting the heater warm up. Then, with the headlights dim to minimize the glare off the fog, she started down the narrow country road.

It was slow going, and Elly told herself to relax and take her time. The fog ebbed and swirled around the car, but she could still make out the edges of the road as well as several yards of pavement in front of her. She would be safe enough if she didn't rush.

The lights of the Palmer's farmhouse disappeared after a short distance, and then there was only the reflected glare of the car's headlights. Elly turned on the radio for company. The road had no other traffic.

She was singing along to one of her favorite country and western songs when the car's engine sputtered and died. Elly let the vehicle drift to the side of the road. Stifling a small anxiety attack, she shut off both the heater and the radio and tried to restart the engine. It became clear very quickly that the task was hopeless. She seemed to be out of gas.

The next thing that became clear was that the only way to get home was to walk. Elly took a long time reaching that decision. The prospect was not a pleasant one. Briefly she considered hiking back toward the Palmers' and then decided that she was about equidistant from her home and that of her friends. She might as well head home.

One of these days, Elly promised herself as she climbed reluctantly out of the car and buttoned her parka, she was going to remember to carry a flashlight in the glove compartment. Things like this probably never happened to Jess. But if they did he'd have been better prepared to handle them.

"One of the advantages of not being married," Elly lectured herself bracingly as she started down the forbidding road. "You won't have to listen to any men yell at you when you get home a little late tonight." You had to look on the bright side.

Jess almost pounced on the phone when it rang that evening in his Portland apartment. He'd been trying to get hold of Elly since six o'clock and had been increasingly frustrated over her failure to answer the phone. She was almost always home when he called. He realized he'd begun to take the fact for granted. In what he knew Elly would refer to as typical male fashion, frustration had turned into irritation, which was rapidly metamorphosing into outright anger.

What Elly wouldn't have guessed, and Jess knew he didn't want to admit, was that the anger was being fed by a fear he dared not put into words. By the time he picked up the receiver, however, his voice was dark and rough with the combination of emotions.

"Mr. Winter, this is Mary at your service."

His answering service. Elly never used that number unless she couldn't reach him at home. He'd been home all evening. Jess closed his eyes briefly as the strange anger in him threatened to increase.

"Go ahead, Mary," he said to the faceless woman he'd never met but who faithfully answered his work number and relayed messages.

"You just had a call from a man who refused to leave his name. He said you'd know who it was." Mary's tone said she strongly disapproved of callers who wouldn't leave proper information.

Jess's fingers locked on the receiver. "Read it to me."

"He said to tell you it was going to be an interesting night on the coast and that he'll have her home by morning."

Jess stared blankly at the white vase full of some sort of tall, artificial grass fronds that stood against the far wall of his living room. He'd never liked the vase or the dull-colored grass, but it had been too much trouble to get rid of it. After all, he'd told himself on countless occasions, he'd be moving soon. He'd be living with Elly, who always kept plenty of fresh flowers and live plants in her home.

"Mr. Winter? Did you get that, sir?"

"Yes, Mary. I got it. Thank you." Very carefully Jess replaced the phone. He had to move carefully or he knew he might fracture the tough plastic between his fingers.

Carrington. The secret fear he hadn't wanted to acknowledge had become real with a vengeance.

The hell of it was, he thought as the fury and fear battled within him, he didn't even know where to start looking. Carrington could have taken Elly anywhere. Women went with him so easily, like moths to a flame.

Jess stood in the middle of his sophisticated off-white living room and thought of his sweet, gentle Elly under Carrington's spell. Quite suddenly, Jess realized he would go out of his mind if he spent the night here in Portland.

He had to go to the coast. He had to be waiting at Elly's home in the morning when Carrington brought her back. He had to see it with his own eyes; had to see Elly mussed and rumpled from a night in Carrington's arms. Then he would tear Damon Carrington apart.

Elly heard the faint sound of a car's engine before she had gone more than a couple hundred feet along the road. She glanced over her shoulder and caught the glare of headlights moving slowly through the swirling fog. Relief swept through her as she turned and started back. Chances were she would know the other driver and he or she would be happy to give her a lift home. It was a wonderful thing living in a small community where you knew your neighbors, Elly thought happily.

She was never quite certain what vague instinct made her decide to identify the vehicle before she darted out into the road to hail it. Perhaps it was the knowledge that not everyone on this road might be familiar or perhaps it was the general eeriness of the swirling fog. A woman had to take a few precautions, she reminded herself, even out here in the boondocks. Jess was always lecturing her along those lines. But, then, he tended to harp on things like that a lot.

Still, she would just make sure that her potential rescuer was someone she knew.

The fog concealed her easily enough as Elly scrambled down into the ditch beside the road and up the other side. There she stood behind the cover of roadside brush and a small clump of trees and watched as the oncoming headlights slowed and then stopped beside her car. She squinted, trying to make out the color of the other vehicle. It wasn't Jim Palmer's beat up red pickup, that was for certain. From what she could see of the car beyond the glaring lights, it looked sleek and sporty. A Porsche, perhaps.

No one she knew drove a Porsche.

Then the sportscar's door opened and a man climbed out of the front seat. Elly identified him even before the headlights illuminated Damon Carrington's blond head as he walked around the front of his car. She froze in the shelter of the brush the way a small animal freezes in the presence of its natural enemy.

Elly was suddenly very grateful she hadn't brought along a flashlight. Carrington might have seen the small beam moving along the road as he'd approached her car.

He walked to the front door of her little compact and peered into the window. A moment later he reached for the handle and yanked it open.

"Elly?"

Her name was chillingly audible in the still night. Elly crouched lower behind the brush, huddling and praying he wouldn't decide to search the nearby terrain.

"Elly? It's me, Damon Carrington. Looks like you had car trouble. I can give you a lift home. Where are you?"

He was just calling to her on the hunch she might still be in the vicinity, Elly thought as she reassured herself. He couldn't know for certain. In another moment he would have to assume that she had abandoned her car much earlier and was already quite a way down the road.

"Elly?" Some of the pleasant, helpfulness of his tone was fading, to be replaced by impatience. Damon walked a few paces down the road in front of the cars, peering into the fog. He didn't glance toward the side or up into the brush beyond the ditch. He was assuming she had continued walking straight down the road.

A logical assumption, Elly admitted to herself. It was exactly what she had done.

"Elly!"

After that last call, Damon apparently decided he was wasting his time. He swung around and headed back toward his car.

Elly watched in relief as he slid inside the Porsche and switched on the engine. The car moved slowly, partly because of the fog, of course, but also because he was probably watching for her, Elly decided. A moment later the sleek car slipped into the fog and disappeared.

She was getting paranoid and it was all Jess Winter's fault.

Shaking her head, Elly straightened from behind the brush and leaped nimbly down into the roadside ditch. Then she darted up the other side and resumed her cold, lonely walk.

It was idiotic to have hidden herself from Carrington like that. She should have been glad of the ride he was offering. Even now she could have been luxuriating in the warmth of the Porsche's front seat. Instead she was stuck with a long walk home. Ridiculous.

But Elly knew in her heart that if she had to make the choice again, she would do the same thing. Jess had warned her to stay away from Damon Carrington because he was wary of the younger man's effect on women. Elly had no fear of Carrington in that sense. She felt absolutely no attraction to the man. But she did fear Carrington's effect on the man she loved. She'd rather walk home in the fog than take a free ride from the man Jess hated.

Not that Jess was ever likely to find out about to-night's odd events, Elly thought as she finally came in sight of the welcoming light from her front porch. It was best he never did. He would put his own construction on things. Then he might go out and do something quite violent. Elly shuddered.

Wearily she tramped the last couple of hundred yards. The fog had lifted a little, but the air had grown colder. A chilled wind was starting up from the sea. The jeans she was wearing provided little protection for her legs, and they were beginning to feel quite numb as she approached her house.

Elly bent her head against the biting breeze, and thus failed to see the other car in her driveway until she almost bumped into it.

For an instant, panic gripped her as she raised her head to see the sleek lines of a pale-white vehicle. In the next instant she realized it wasn't a Porsche. It was Jess's Jaguar sedan.

Cold, damp and weary, Elly paused beside the car, staring down at it. She couldn't figure out what it was doing in her driveway in the middle of the week. Jess had said nothing about driving over to the coast before Friday. With a sigh she continued toward the porch, climbing the old wooden steps as if they were small mountains.

The door opened before she could dig her key out of her leather shoulder bag, and Elly found herself staring up into Jess Winter's taut, savage face. In the harsh light of the porch fixture, his eyes were the color of the fog that had shrouded the road behind her. The tension in him was lethal.

"Elly."

She blinked, alarmed by the harshness of her name on his lips. She drew a deep breath and stepped forward, pushing past him into her warm, inviting hall. "Well, of course it's Elly. I live here, remember? What in the world are you doing here on a Wednesday, Jess? You always do things on schedule and you're not scheduled to be here until Friday. My God, it's cold out there. My legs are absolutely numb. I need a hot shower and a cup of hot chocolate. You wouldn't believe what happened to me tonight. I ran out of gas. And don't give me any lectures on the subject because I could have sworn I had plenty of fuel. I just filled the tank on Monday at Pete's service station and I've hardly driven twenty or thirty miles since . . ."

"Elly!"

She swung around. "What is it, Jess?"

"Are you all right?"

"I'm fine. Just a little cold. Why shouldn't I be all right? It was a long walk but other than that . . ."

Jess stepped forward, his hands coming up to clamp around her shoulders. Oddly she could feel the tension in him and it frightened her. Elly realized she'd never seen Jess in quite this mood.

"I had a message from Carrington," he began grimly.

"Carrington!" She stared at him in shocked disbelief. "Why on earth would he contact you?"

"To tell me you were spending the night with him, and that he would bring you home in the morning."

Images of Damon Carrington prowling through the fog, searching for her, rose up in Elly's mind and took on new, menacing significance. "I was at the Palmers' tonight, Jess. You remember I told you about the potluck? I ran out of gas on the way home and had to walk."

"I can see that." His eyes moved over her, taking in the fog-dampened hair and parka, the mud-splattered shoes and the breeze-whipped color of her cheeks. Suddenly he pulled her fiercely into his arms. "Hell, Elly. I can *see* that."

Elly thought he would crush the breath out of her body. The driving urgency in him was totally new to her. She wasn't certain how to handle it.

"I would have killed him, Elly. I would have strangled him with my bare hands if he had brought you home in the morning."

"Then started in on me?" Elly tried to lift her head so that she could look up into his face, but Jess continued to crush her against his hard body.

"Elly..."

"Jess," she whispered, wrapping her arms around his neck, "how could you think I would go with him?"

"You don't know him, Elly."

"I know one thing for certain about him: He's not the man I want. Furthermore, I resent your thinking that I'm some empty-headed female who's an easy victim for any good-looking man who happens to come along. I'm an adult human being, Jess, and I'm quite capable of picking and choosing my acquaintances on the basis of something besides their physical appearance!"

"Calm down, Elly."

"I will not calm down! Why should I? I've had a miserable walk home, and I arrive to find some brute on my doorstep who thinks I'm totally unable to run my own life. Your faith in me is hardly flattering, Jess. In fact, I get the distinct impression you don't have much trust in me at all. Hardly a good way to begin a marriage. The more I think about it, the more I'm convinced we're not going to make it together, after all. I want someone who has some respect for my integrity and my brains. Furthermore—"

"Elly, hush."

"Why should I hush? In addition to integrity and brains, I've also got a mouth."

"You can say that again!"

Before Elly could protest further, Jess stopped her tirade with the most fundamental approach of all. He covered her mouth with his own, and this time his kiss wasn't the casual sort she had come to expect from him.

His hands were already moving in her hair, even as his tongue surged possessively between her teeth.

This time, Elly knew, Jess intended to set his seal on her. He was going to take her to bed.

For the first time since she had begun to acknowledge her love for him, Elly was afraid of what would happen if she let him make love to her.

Five

The fear and uncertainty were real, but neither could prevail against the desperate need for reassurance Elly read in Jess's eyes. It was odd, she thought fleetingly as he gathered her into his arms, for the past two months she had been the one seeking reassurance, eventually trying for it on a physical basis. Tonight Jess hungered for it.

But there was a sharp, inescapable difference in the underlying motives. Elly had sought assurance of his love, some indication of a passion and need that matched her own. Tonight Jess was seeking only assurance of her commitment to him. She would be a fool if she forgot that fundamental distinction. But reason and caution faded next to her overwhelming desire to give Jess what he seemed to need.

"Elly," he muttered against her mouth, "I should have done this a long time ago. I should have realized that with a woman like you this is a way to be sure. I handled it all wrong. I see that now.''

"Handled what wrong? Jess, I don't—'' But his tongue probed boldly into her mouth once more, and Elly moaned softly beneath the sensual onslaught.

His strong hands slid down her back, blunt fingers kneading her muscles with undisguised pleasure. When he reached her waist Jess lifted her, pulling her up into the urgent hardness of his lower body.

At least there was no doubt that he wanted her, Elly thought dazedly. She clung to that knowledge as fiercely as she clung to him. If she could make him want her badly enough, perhaps he would let himself love her.

"Sweetheart, you're still cold. I'm going to take you upstairs and warm you.'' Jess cradled her in his arms as he started toward the stairs.

Elly felt the strength in him and relaxed into it. She nestled her head against his shoulder as he carried her up the stairs and down the hall to her bedroom. There in the shadows he set her on her feet while he reached down to yank the comforter out of the way. When he turned back to her she smiled tremulously

"You're very sweet, Elly Trent. Very soft. And I think the time has come for me to take what you're offering.'' He let his fingertip trail inside the collar of her shirt, following the opening until he came to the first button. Then, quite deliberately, Jess began unfastening the buttons. As he worked his way down to the hem of the shirt, he let his knuckles glide teasingly over her skin.

By the time the shirt hung open, Elly was trembling. She whispered his name a little brokenly and caught his hand. Lifting it to her lips, she kissed his palm with a gentle passion that made him catch his breath.

"When I think of the two months I've wasted!" Jess shook his head once, wonderingly and his mouth curved in brief, wry amusement. "Never again, honey. After tonight you're going to be in my bed every night I can arrange it. And after we're married that will be full-time."

"I'm glad you want me," Elly said simply, her eyes luminous in the shadows. "So glad." She stepped out of her shoes.

He pushed the shirt to one side, uncovering a breast. "The important thing is that you want me. Tonight you're going to show me just how much, aren't you?"

He lifted his gaze to meet hers, and for a blazing moment Elly read the intent in him. "Jess, this isn't a contest. There's nothing to prove."

"Yes, there is." He stroked her nipple, watching it harden beneath his touch. "Yes, there is." The satisfaction was plain on his face. When she shivered slightly, he became impatient and pushed the shirt off completely. Then he captured her wrist and guided her hand to the buttons of his own garment. "Help me undress, Elly."

Obediently she began easing him out of his shirt. It was a difficult task because her fingers were a little shaky. Jess seemed to enjoy her awkwardness. He watched her slow progress with a curiously intent expression.

"Now," he murmured as the shirt fell to his feet, "put your arms around my neck and hold me. I want to feel you, honey."

Slowly Elly did as he instructed, stifling a small gasp when her breasts brushed against the crisp curly hair of his chest.

"Harder," Jess ordered softly, his lips in her hair.

"Oh, Jess." Elly turned her face into his bare shoulder, shuddering as she pressed closer. Her nipples felt hard and almost unbearably sensitized. The feel of his rough skin against them bordered on the painful. "It hurts," she breathed.

"Does it?"

"Almost."

He laughed softly. "Almost isn't the same thing as actually hurting. If it ever really hurts, tell me. I'll stop. The last thing I ever want to do, Elly, is cause you pain."

She curled her arms more trustingly around his neck, and the next thing Elly was aware of was Jess's fingers moving between their bodies. He searched for and found the snap of her jeans. Then he was pushing the denims down over her hips, letting them drop to her feet. She felt his hands on her buttocks, clenching and unclenching tenderly. Only her striped cotton briefs shielded her now.

"Jess, I'm going crazy." She pressed more closely against him and heard his growled response.

"That's just the way I want you. Let yourself go, Elly. Show me how much you want me."

She snuggled closer, dropping her hands to his waist so that she could finish undressing him. But she fumbled so with the zipper that Jess finally stepped back to do the job himself.

"Get into bed, honey. You're still too cold."

She crawled between the sheets, pulling the comforter up to cover her breasts and watched as Jeff stepped out of the rest of his clothes. In the shadowed light, his body looked lean and smoothly muscled, and when he turned to face her the hard evidence of his desire was so blatant Elly's glance instinctively moved away from the sight. Determinedly she kept her gaze on his face as he pulled aside the comforter and slid into bed.

"Why the shyness, Elly? We're going to be married soon. You want me. I want you. It's all very simple. It would have been even simpler if I'd come to my senses earlier." Jess put his hand on her flat stomach and let his fingers trail beneath the elastic edge of her briefs. "Lift up, honey and let me take these off."

"Jess, I'm sorry you were worried about me tonight."

"I know you're sorry. I could see it in your eyes. You have such beautiful eyes, sweetheart. My God, I want you. I've been walking your living-room floor until I thought I would go out of my mind. Now you're here and you're safe. I don't think I've ever been more grateful for anything in my life than I was to see you come through that door tonight. If Carrington had brought you back with him in the morning, I—"

"Hush," Elly whispered. "It didn't happen that way. I would never let it happen that way."

Elly's briefs came off in his hands, and he dropped them casually beside the bed. Then Jess let his palm glide up the length of her leg until he reached her thigh.

"Open up, sweetheart. Let me touch you. I want to feel you get hot and damp for me." He bent his head and slightly caught her nipple between his lips.

"Jess!" The exquisite sensation made her arch her head back over his arm, and without any conscious thought her legs parted for him. Elly speared her fingers into the darkness of his hair, gripping with sudden urgency as he probed her softness.

"I can't believe I denied myself this for two months. You're on fire, aren't you, Elly?"

"You're tormenting me," she protested, sinking her nails into his shoulders as he continued to stroke her. "And I think you're doing it deliberately."

Jess raised his head to look down into her eyes. "Maybe I am," he admitted quietly. "I like seeing you all soft and helpless. I like seeing how much you want me."

Through the gathering storm of her arousal, Elly caught the hidden meaning behind his words. "Because it makes you feel in control? Jess, please, I don't want our lovemaking to be a . . . a matter of control."

"What do you want it to be?" He seemed unconcerned as he leaned down again to feather her throat with kisses.

"It should be a giving thing," she tried to say, but her words were almost lost in her throat as he did something incredibly erotic between her legs. "Jess, please . . . !"

"I agree, sweetheart. I want you to give yourself to me. No argument. Ah, sweet Elly, you're delicious, do you know that? If only you could see yourself right now. You're losing yourself in my arms. You're going out of control."

He was right. Elly decided there was no point trying to fight her reaction to him. The passion he aroused in her was unique, unlike anything she had ever experienced. She loved him. What more did a woman need to strip her of self-control? With a soft moan, Elly gave herself up to the swirling excitement of Jess's lovemaking. She slid her hands eagerly over his body, exploring the lean, muscled contours until she came into contact with the rock hard shaft of his manhood. Jess's eyes momentarily narrowed until they were almost closed.

"Oh, God, Elly, yes. I want you. I can't remember ever wanting a woman like this."

She sensed that the admission was almost unconscious on his part. Jess, too, was slipping out of control, and the realization set fire to Elly's own excitement. She put her lips to his chest, nipping him delicately with her sharp little teeth.

"This isn't painful; it's *almost* painful, right?" she dared as he sucked in his breath.

"Thinking of crossing the line?"

"I wouldn't dream of it."

Jess regarded her with burning eyes. "I know. I think I've known all along. You're gentle, Elly. Probably too gentle for your own good. But it doesn't matter now. I'll take care of you."

"Jess?"

"Hush, darling." He eased her over onto her back and lowered himself slowly along the length of her. "I'm going to take you now. I'm going to watch you melt in my arms. You said this should be a giving thing. So give, Elly. All of yourself. I'll take good care of the gift."

She was too far gone along the sensual road to struggle with the message in his words. Elly closed her eyes and wrapped her arms around Jess's neck. She could feel his hard, blunt shaft waiting between her thighs, and when he used his hand to push her legs farther apart she didn't resist. Then he surged against her, and she cried out as he buried himself deep into her body. Jess paused, his body throbbing.

"Painful or almost?" he grated, holding himself very still above her.

"Just almost. Oh, Jess, I've never felt this way before."

"You've led a sheltered life." But she could hear the satisfaction in him. "I can see that." She opened her eyes as he began to move within her. "I'm glad."

His face was a taut mask of barely controlled masculine urgency. He held her so tightly Elly couldn't tell which of them was exuding the fine perspiration that slicked their skin. She felt Jess's hands under her hips, lifting her, guiding her as he increased the pace of the lovemaking.

The strange tension in Elly began to tighten and condense. She was unaware of the way her legs wrapped around Jess's waist as she closed her eyes again. The powerful driving rhythm was dominating her senses, and she could only respond to its demands. She was alive with the knowledge that the man who held her so fiercely was the man she loved, and when the shimmering climax shook her, Elly could no longer avoid saying the words.

"Jess, oh, Jess, I love you, love you, love you..."

Jess lifted his head to watch her face as she surrendered to the force of their mutual passion. He realized that the words were the finishing touch. They made it all perfect. She was his in a way no other woman had ever been. No one else had ever given herself so sweetly and completely. She loved him. She *loved* him.

Then he couldn't think at all as his own satisfaction washed over him. The release seemed endless and infinite, and at the conclusion he sprawled heavily on Elly's softness. For a long moment he lay still, luxuriating in the feel of her and then, reluctantly, he rolled to one side. When he gathered her against him, she opened her eyes and met his gaze. He stared down at her, drinking in the sight of her tawny-gold eyes. Then he smiled slightly and picked up a trailing braid that had come free of the coronet she normally wore. He toyed with it as he leaned down to brush her lips with his own.

"No doubt about it. I was a fool to wait this long."

"Why did you wait, Jess?" The tawny eyes were unexpectedly serious.

He shrugged, no longer interested in his own motivations. He couldn't begin to explain that a part of him had been wary of the kind of passion he sensed he would find with Elly. Now that he'd found it and discovered there was absolutely nothing threatening about it, that it was, in fact, fantastic, Jess saw no reason to go into the subject. "As you've often noticed, I tend to do things on schedule."

"And you haven't had time until tonight to fit me into your schedule?"

"Hey," he said chuckling, "I thought you'd appreciate not being rushed. Don't I get any points for gentlemanly behavior?"

"It made me nervous." She dropped her eyes to study his chest.

"Because you were beginning to be afraid I didn't want you at all. Then when you decided to take things into your own hands last weekend I blew it by seeing that prowler at the window. That was probably Carrington, the bastard. One of these days I'm going to have to do something about him before his mischief gets dangerous."

"You haven't answered my question," Elly persisted.

Jess sighed. "You mean about why I was such a gentleman for two months?"

"Yes."

"It was because I wanted to be sure of you in other ways, first. You're sweet and sensible and intelligent. I wanted you to see that we could make a good marriage together, that we were right for each other. I didn't want to be accused of using sex to push you into anything you didn't really want." It sounded reasonable to his own ears.

"Because someone once used sex to push you into a marriage you later regretted?"

"That's not going to be a problem with us, though, is it, Elly? You love me. You want to marry me. You've loved me and you've wanted to marry me all along."

"Yes."

He tipped up her chin, enjoying the honesty in her eyes. "I should have known. I should have guessed how deeply you felt. If I had, I wouldn't have waited two months to make love to you."

"Now you know how I feel," she began carefully.

"Umm." He felt the satisfaction welling up in him, and knew it probably showed in his eyes. Jess didn't try to hide it. There was no need.

"I'd like to know how you feel, Jess." Elly studied him intently.

"Damned good." He stretched and yawned.

"That's not what I meant."

Something in her persistent tone finally got through to him. He blinked lazily. "What do you mean?"

She swallowed, seeking the right words. "I want to know if you love me," Elly whispered starkly.

Jess experienced the first flicker of uneasiness. She looked so serious and concerned. Tenderly he played with her braid. "Elly, honey, I'm going to marry you. I'll take care of you. I think you trust me, and you know that I want you. I know for certain that you want me. Isn't that enough for you?"

"I don't know. Is falling in love with me anywhere in sight on that schedule of yours? Or is this all I'm going to get?"

The uneasiness began to change into anger. "What, exactly, do you want from me, Elly?"

"I want you to tell me that you love me," she said with stubborn pride. "That you're giving yourself to me as completely as I'm prepared to give myself to you. That you're passionately, irrevocably, inescapably, deliriously in love with me!"

"Why?"

❧ IT'S A ❧

SILHOUETTE HONEYMOON
A SWEETHEART
OF A FREE OFFER!

FOUR NEW
SILHOUETTE DESIRE NOVELS—FREE!

Take a "Silhouette Honeymoon" with four exciting romances—yours FREE from Silhouette Desire. Each of these hot-off-the-press novels brings you all the passion and tenderness of today's greatest love stories...your free passport to a bright new world of love and adventure!

But wait...there's <u>even more</u> to this great offer!

SPECIAL EXTRAS—FREE!

You'll get our free monthly newsletter, packed with news on your favorite writers, upcoming books, even recipes from your favorite authors.

Best of all, you'll receive romance novels that go *beyond* the others...novels written for the woman who wants a more provocative, passion-filled reading experience.

MONEY-SAVING HOME DELIVERY!

Send for your Silhouette Desire novels and enjoy the <u>convenience</u> of previewing six new books every month, delivered right to your home. Each book is yours for only $1.95—<u>30¢ less per book</u> than what you pay in stores! Great savings plus total convenience add up to a sweetheart of a deal for <u>you</u>!

START YOUR SILHOUETTE HONEYMOON TODAY—
JUST COMPLETE, DETACH & MAIL YOUR FREE OFFER CARD!

FILL OUT THIS POSTPAID CARD AND MAIL TODAY!

SILHOUETTE DESIRE®

FREE OFFER CARD

**PLACE HEART
STICKER HERE**

**4 FREE
BOOKS**

**PLUS AN
EXTRA BONUS
MYSTERY GIFT!**

**FREE
HOME
DELIVERY!**

☐ YES! Please send me my four SILHOUETTE DESIRE romances, free, along with my free Mystery Gift! Then send me six new SILHOUETTE DESIRE novels every month, as they come off the presses, and bill me just $1.95 per book (30¢ less than retail), with no extra charges for shipping and handling. If I am not completely satisfied, I may return a shipment and cancel at any time. The free books and Mystery Gift remain mine to keep

NAME_____
(please print)

ADDRESS_____

CITY_____

STATE_____ ZIP_____

Terms and prices subject to change. Your enrollment is subject to acceptance by Silhouette Books.
SILHOUETTE DESIRE is a registered trademark.

CDD825

Limited Time Offer!

Make sure you get this great FREE OFFER—act today!

BUSINESS REPLY CARD

FIRST CLASS PERMIT NO. 194 CLIFTON, N.J.

Postage will be paid by addressee

Silhouette Books
120 Brighton Road
P.O. Box 5084
Clifton, NJ 07015-9956

NO POSTAGE
NECESSARY
IF MAILED
IN THE
UNITED STATES

"Why!" She freed herself to sit up against the pillows. "Why? Because that's the way this whole thing is supposed to work. That's what getting married is all about. I love you. I'd like some assurance that you love me."

He eyed her for a long moment, taking in the sight of her emotions so openly displayed in her face. "Last weekend you said you wanted the assurance that I could feel genuine passion for you. I've given you that assurance and now you want more. How much more, Elly?"

She flinched as if he had struck her. "That's not fair, Jess. I'm only asking that the man who claims he wants to marry me also does me the honor of telling me he loves me. But you're not going to do that, are you?" She edged toward the side of the bed, her eyes blazing. All the warmth of the passionate aftermath of their lovemaking had changed to feminine resentment.

"Elly, come back here. Where the hell do you think you're going?" Alarmed and irritated, Jess sat up.

"You're afraid to let yourself love me, aren't you?" she challenged, stumbling to her feet beside the bed. She dragged the comforter with her. "After that disaster with Marina Carrington, you're not about to risk loving another woman."

"You don't know what the hell you're talking about! I felt a lot of things for Marina, but not love." Jess exploded off the bed, catching Elly by the wrist because she would have darted toward the bathroom. "Now calm down and stop throwing a temper tantrum or so help me I'll..."

"You'll what? Beat me?" She glared at him.

Jess relaxed, his mouth curving slightly. "No, honey, I won't beat you. I'll take you back to bed and make love to you all over again. This time I'll try to do the job right so that you don't come out of it spitting like a scalded cat.''

She was beyond caution now. "Maybe you can't do the job right. The only right way to make love to me, Jess Winter, is to *be* in love with me.''

"Damn you, Elly!'' Unexpectedly Jess lost his own temper. Gray eyes darkened with masculine intent. Clamping her around the waist, he lifted her so that she was eye to eye with him. Hastily she braced herself with her palms on his shoulders. Her gaze was gold with the fire of her feelings. "You little witch, I'll teach you to provoke me. I'm going to lay you back and make love to you until you admit I not only give you what you need in bed, but that you won't ever want it from anyone else! Do you hear me, woman?''

Elly heard. She heard all too clearly. She paled at the words. *Witch*. She'd heard him call her a witch, and with that all the fight went out of her. She was not another Marina, not another witch who would deliberately bait and torment him. The fear that she had acted in a way that reminded him of the other woman swept through her. Impulsively Elly threw her arms around his neck, sinking into him, pleading with him silently to forget the outburst.

"I hear you, Jess. You don't have to prove it.'' She smiled tentatively into his shoulder. "But if you're intent on doing so, I won't argue.''

"Elly?''

"I love you, Jess.''

His hands softened on her. "I know, honey, I know.'' He set her gently on the bed and came down beside her, gathering her closely. "I'll take care of you and your love, Elly Trent. I swear it.''

He didn't call her a witch again. As she lay in bed a long while later, Elly reminded herself that Jess hadn't called Marina's name or seen her face while he was making love. If the other woman still haunted him, at least he hadn't brought her out into the open tonight. As she snuggled down into the comforting heat of his body and closed her eyes, Elly told herself that there was no way Jess could have made love with such passionate intensity if he'd been thinking of another woman.

She thought briefly of explaining exactly what had happened on the lonely, foggy road that night but decided there was nothing to be gained except a violent confrontation. The last thing she wanted to do was involve Jess in another such scene. She had no doubt that he would put the worst possible interpretation on the situation if she were to tell him how Damon Carrington had conveniently happened along shortly after her car had run out of gas. He might have been right, she admitted sleepily. Combined with the evidence of the mischief-making message Damon had apparently sent to Jess, that business out on the road was a little too much of a coincidence.

Had Carrington really thought that he could casually pick her up, take her somewhere for the night and seduce her? Had he actually thought she would allow him to do it? The man must have an ego the size of a football field. Well, she had proven she could take care of herself where Carrington was concerned. There was no point bringing in the heavy guns and risking genuine violence. Elly went cold at the thought. It seemed much smarter to keep Jess and Damon separated.

Just as it had the last time Jess had spent the night, the phone rang early the next morning. Elly blinked herself awake even as Jess shoved back the covers.

"Damn," he said. I'll get it. We're going to have to start leaving your phone unplugged at night." He paced toward the door, not bothering to collect any clothes en route. Arrogantly unconcerned with his own nakedness, he stalked out into the hall, heading for the stairs.

Elly watched him leave, bemused by the novelty of waking up with a man in her bed. She really had led a quiet life until Jess came along, she thought, yawning. All things considered it had remained fairly quiet for a couple of months after he had come along, too! Things had definitely changed last night.

She could hear his voice faintly as he responded to the caller. Elly was content to stretch grandly and take her time about heading for a shower, until she realized that Jess's muffled tones were sounding cold and impatient.

Frowning, Elly sat up and pushed back the comforter, trying to listen. When she heard the name *Trentco,* she was jolted into full wakefulness. Hastily she scrambled out of bed, grabbed her robe and started for the stairs. She was in time to catch the last of Jess's conversation with her Aunt Clara. He was speaking crisply, with more than a faint trace of aloof arrogance.

"That won't be necessary, Mrs. Gaines. I've got all the resources I need at my disposal. Advising people in situations such as this is my business and I'm good at it." There was a pause while Clara Gaines apparently tried to argue. "Don't bother. Elly will have me to consult. I'll be handling the matter for her, and I'll make sure she reaches the right decision. For the record, as her consultant in this deal, I'd like to point out that I don't want her hounded anymore. In other words, no more seven

A.M. phone calls. We high-priced financial wizards get irritated by early-morning calls.''

"Jess!'' Elly stood clutching the lapels of her robe, trying to get his attention. "Jess, get off the phone. Let me talk to her. This isn't your concern.''

But Jess ignored her as he responded to Aunt Clara's next remark. "I wouldn't worry too much about her offbeat life-style, Mrs. Gaines. It doesn't impact her ability to vote her shares in Trentco, and that's the only aspect of it you have to concern yourself with, isn't it? I'll look forward to meeting you next Monday at the stockholders' meeting. What's that? Of course, I'll be attending as Elly's adviser. Should be interesting. Good-bye, Mrs. Gaines.''

He threw the phone carelessly back down into its cradle and turned to eye Elly with an indulgently lifted brow. "What's the matter, honey? You look as if one of those sharks you're always worrying about just swam ashore.''

"Jess, you shouldn't have interfered. You have no right to involve yourself. What was all that nonsense about your being my consultant? This is very messy, very complicated family business and I really don't think you should just, well, invite yourself into it.''

"I realize it involves your family, Elly,'' he said placatingly, "but it also involves you, and it involves business finance. Both are areas in which I'm an expert. That gives me the right to act as your consultant.''

"Expert! You're not an expert on me, for heaven's sake!'' She gestured wildly, lost control of the robe and had to make a quick grab for it, which effectively ruined the impact of the gesture. "You think one night in bed somehow gives you the right to make my business decisions for me? Well, you're wrong. I've been dealing with this family for a long time, and I can handle the situation on my own. I don't need any high-priced financial consultant taking over for me. Stay out of this, Jess. If I want your advice, I'll ask for it.''

He studied her for a long moment, taking in the ruffled chaos of her hair, the comfortable old robe and the militant gleam in her eyes.

"Elly, don't be ridiculous. Why should you walk into that meeting alone on Monday? It's going to be you against the rest of them, and they're going to be furious if you don't vote the way they want you to vote. Why face it all by yourself when you've got me?''

"It won't be just me. Harrigan's on my side,'' she reminded him huffily.

"Oh, yes, Harrigan. The CEO. That reminds me, I want to give him a call this afternoon.'' Absently Jess glanced around the room until he spotted a pencil and a notepad. Bending down, he jotted himself a quick message and dropped the pencil.

"Jess, please, listen to me.'' Elly decided to stop arguing and try the reasonable approach. "Harrigan and I will be fine. Aunt Clara and the gang aren't going to chew me up, you know. There's absolutely nothing they can do if I decide to vote against them.''

"They can put a hell of a lot of pressure on you, make you feel guilty, make you distrust your own judgment. Believe me, Elly, I've seen people in this kind of situation. Even the normally mild-tempered ones can turn into cobras if they see profits slipping through their fingers.''

The reasonable approach gave way to pleading. "Please, Jess, don't get involved. Can't you understand? I don't want you involved!''

He stepped forward and drew her into his arms. "I understand what you're saying. What I can't figure out is why you're saying it. I'm your lover, and soon I'm going to be your husband. Why are you trying to keep me out of family business?''

Elly tried desperately to find the words to explain her fears, but in the end she couldn't bring herself to say them aloud. Maybe Jess didn't see what was happening, but she certainly did and it terrified her.

She could see him letting himself being dragged into an unpleasant, potentially nasty family-business situation just as he had been when he'd married Marina Carrington. True, the circumstances were different, but the essense of the situation was the same. It hinged on money. Jess had already been burned on the subject of family and money. She vividly remembered what he'd told her about having to bail Damon Carrington out of one financial disaster after another.

Jess didn't even realize how awkward things could get. If *Trentco* wasn't sold, Aunt Clara and the rest would probably insist that Elly's ''financial consultant'' offer a great deal of free financial advice to the firm. From their point of view, he would have been responsible for keeping them from realizing a quick, sure profit. He would therefore be expected to compensate by ensuring a long-term profit.

If he chose not to cooperate, there would be endless recriminations, badgering and pleas. If he did cooperate, there would be demands, phone calls, arguments and petty complaints. And there were certain members of the Trent family who were not above asking for a loan. Shades of Damon Carrington. The unpleasantness would never go away because families never go away. Elly knew that for a fact. She had moved as far from her relations as possible, and she still couldn't escape from them.

Last night, when she had provoked Jess, he had called her a witch, the same term he used so disparagingly for his dead ex-wife. If she allowed him to get involved in her family financial problems, how long would it be before he would resent the ceaseless demands? How long before he would realize she was causing him as much trouble as the Carringtons had once caused him?

Elly realized with a sense of nervous dread that she was fighting for Jess's love. She wanted nothing to remind him of the past. If she was to have any chance at all of getting him to take the risk of loving her, she would have to shield him from certain elements in her world.

Above all, she must not say or do the things that would make him think of her as another witch, and she must not allow him to be pulled into another nasty, vicious family-business situation.

"Jess," she said with grave dignity, "this doesn't concern you. Please don't worry about it or about me. I'll be fine." She turned on her heel and climbed the stairs to her bedroom.

Six

Maybe he'd come down too heavily on her this morning when he'd warned Elly again about steering clear of Carrington. Jess's eyes narrowed as he guided the Jaguar toward Portland and thought of Elly's uncertain mood.

No, he'd given her the lecture just before leaving, and she'd been in an odd temper long before that.

Perhaps she was upset by the unexpected manner in which their relationship had been altered overnight. They were lovers now. Jess tasted the words with a sense of deep satisfaction. About time. He should never have waited this long. There had been nothing to be wary of, after all. He still felt totally in control of the affair. More so, to be perfectly honest, than he had before making love to her.

He had Elly's sweetly passionate nature to thank for his sense of sureness about her. She gave herself so completely, so trustingly, all softness and heat and feminine need. Jess's hands tightened abruptly on the wheel as the images floated again through his mind. Wryly amused at his own reaction to the memories, he forced himself to relax and go back to the main problem.

Elly was trying to resist some element of their relationship, and he couldn't figure out why. It wasn't the sexual side of things. He'd proven that to himself last night. The truth was she hadn't resisted that aspect from the beginning. She would have come to him any time. All he would have had to do was beckon and she would have flown into his arms. He should have started beckoning two months ago. Ah well, live and learn. That angle was settled now, anyway. It wasn't the source of the problem, he felt sure.

So why was she so nervous around him this morning? Why the temper over the way he'd handled the call from Clara Gaines? When he'd told Elly he'd not only be advising her on the Trentco matter, but that he'd accompany her to California, she'd really become withdrawn.

It was that strange withdrawal that annoyed him. It was as if Elly were trying to keep him out of a part of her life. He didn't like it, and what irritated him most was that he didn't understand it. Why fight him in that area when she welcomed him so passionately in others? Jess frowned, automatically bringing the Jag smoothly out of a tight curve, and asked himself what the hell was going on. Whatever it was, he intended to get to the bottom of it soon.

In the meantime he had work to do. Aunt Clara promised to be a real dragon, and the rest of the family probably followed her lead. He'd get in touch with Harrigan, the CEO, as soon as he got back to Portland. There was another task waiting for him this afternoon, too. He wanted to call the very exclusive, very reliable firm of investigators he had hired on Monday.

Elly made one last, weak attempt to stay the inevitable that night when Jess called to tell her the results of his conversation with Matt Harrigan.

"You were right when you said he seemed to know what he's doing, Elly. He's going to use Trentco as a basis for building his reputation as the kind of executive officer who can rescue struggling firms. That's a good incentive. He's more than happy to work on a bonus plan, which means he won't make big money unless he's successful. Seems to have a solid knowledge of Trentco's problems and assets, and last but least, he isn't intimidated by Aunt Clara and the crowd."

Elly listened to the summing up of Matt Harrigan's strong points. A part of her was deeply relieved to know her intuition had been correct. "I'm glad you think he's a good person to have at the helm. Since you're confident of his abilities, you must see there's really no need to go down to California with me. I can handle the meeting."

"Forget it, Elly. I don't want you facing that crowd alone and that's final. Now, I've arranged our flight out of Portland for Saturday afternoon. You can have Sarah Mitchell take over the store for you. You've used her before to cover the place, as I recall. You were going to have her open for you on Monday, anyway. I'm sure she'll be glad of the extra day's work. I'll expect you here in Portland sometime before noon. Don't be late. The plane leaves at one-thirty and I don't want any last-minute snafus."

Elly winced at the stream of directives. There was clearly no stopping Jess. Irritably, she leaned back against the sofa and crossed her jeaned legs on the footstool. She glared at the opposite wall, listening to the list of instructions.

A collection of ivy plants occupied an old wooden bench that was positioned against the wall. The vines cascaded in rich abundance all the way to the floor. From where she was sitting, Elly could see the handle of the paring knife she had again borrowed from the kitchen to use for gardening work. If Jess could have seen it sitting there he would have had a few pithy things to say. *"How many times have I told you, you never know when you're going to need a sharp knife?"* It was probably distinctly juvenile to take this much satisfaction out of having defied him in one small department.

When Jess finally halted to ask if she had it all down, she answered him a little too smoothly. "Yes, sir. I've got it all written in indelible ink on the back of my hand. Be in Portland by noon. Don't be late. Get Sarah to cover the store. Does it occur to you Jess that I managed to survive for thirty years without you to schedule me?"

There was a pause from the other end of the line. Elly had the distinct impression Jess was deciding just how to deal with her unexpected flippancy. She'd probably regret it, herself, later. But right now she was feeling frustrated and a little angry.

"Something wrong with my schedule?" Jess finally asked calmly.

"You know there's nothing wrong with it. It's just the principle of the thing, I guess."

"Elly, why are you so reluctant to let me help you with the Trentco problem?"

She tried to think of a reasonable answer and finally decided to hint at the truth. Taking a deep breath, Elly said quietly, "Has it occurred to you that if you get involved in Trentco at this stage there might be a lot of pressure from Aunt Clara and the gang later? They can be a very demanding bunch, Jess. Very difficult.''

''Is that what's worrying you? Forget it. Aunt Clara and the crowd are bunny rabbits compared to some of the stockholders I've dealt with in the past. Which reminds me. I called your aunt and told her we would be taking her and the others out to dinner Saturday evening.''

Elly jerked upright. ''You did what?''

''You heard me.''

''Jess, that's positively the last thing I feel like doing! You had no right. What's the point, anyway? For heaven's sake, this is my family problem, not yours.''

''I decided it would be a courtesy to gather them together and explain your position and why you were going to vote not to sell. I'll lay out the facts and figures for them.''

''Harrigan and I have already beaten them over the head with facts and figures!''

''That's the whole point,'' Jess said patiently. ''Coming from me, maybe it will make more of an impression.''

Visions of Saturday evening degenerating into a screaming match boggled Elly's mind for a fraught moment or two. Frantically, she tried to think of counter arguments, but Jess was already pursuing another line of thought.

''Do you realize,'' he was saying with a touch of anticipation, ''that this will be the first time you and I have actually gone away together for a weekend? I've spent the past two months driving over to the coast, but you haven't had a chance to grab a small vacation. We'll have a good time, honey.''

''Jess, this is hardly a minivacation!''

"We'll make it one. I've already made the reservation." He named one of the big hotels near Union Square in downtown San Francisco. "I know a couple of great places for dinner and maybe some dancing. Do you dance, Elly?" he added interestedly. "That's something else we haven't done together."

"But, Jess..."

"Don't worry about not having the right clothes. San Francisco's very stylish, of course, but no one's going to notice if you don't look as if you just stepped out of *Vogue*."

"Thanks." Elly could hardly breathe through her fury.

"I'm really looking forward to this, honey," Jess concluded.

"Good night, Jess."

Elly hung up the phone before her temper exploded. Surging to her feet, she paced the comfortable living room until she had managed to work off some of the seething resentment. By the tenth or fifteen trip across the floor, her sense of humor finally began to assert itself. Also her sense of reason.

She had to remember that Jess had never seen her in anything but jeans and the exceedingly casual clothes worn in a small coastal town. As he had just pointed out, they hadn't gone anywhere more sophisticated together. He hadn't intended to be condescending on the phone. He'd been trying to reassure her.

Sweet man.

Sweet man, hell. It would be a pleasure to shake him up a little. Jess Winter was entirely too sure of his own judgments.

Reaching for the phone again, Elly dialed Sarah Mitchell's number. When her friend answered after a couple of rings, Elly burst into speech.

"Sarah, do you want to handle the shop for me on Friday and Saturday as well as Monday?"

"Well, sure, Elly. That's no problem. What's up? Going out of town early?"

"Yes, as a matter of fact. I wanted a chance to do some shopping in Portland before I go to San Francisco."

"Okay. I'll take care of The Natural Choice. You won't get any argument from me. I can use the money; you know that."

"Great. Oh, Sarah?" Elly remembered something. "How did the outing go?"

"You mean with Damon Carrington? Don't ask."

"It didn't work out?" Elly thought of Compass Rose's violent reaction to the man.

"It wasn't that bad, I guess. We went to the section of beach near your place. You know that cove with the big rock sitting in the middle of it?"

"Sure."

"Well, the tide was in, so we couldn't get near the rock to check out the tidepools. The breeze was cold. And Compass Rose had a fit. All in all, not a memorable outing. Haven't seen Damon since."

"Oh. I'm sorry, Sarah."

"It's probably just as well. If you want to know the truth, there was something about him that reminded me a little too much of Mark."

"How's that?"

"You know, all surface glitter and no depth."

"I think that was Ann Palmer's reaction, too," Elly said thoughtfully. "Maybe we country women are a little more astute when it comes to judging men than city boys like to think we are. I know one city male who's going to find out that he's got a few things to learn about a particular country woman."

"Jess?"

"How did you guess?"

Sarah laughed. "A hunch. He's going with you to San Francisco?"

"I can't seem to stop him. The thing is, he's never seen me out of a pair of jeans." Unless you counted the times he'd seen her naked, Elly amended silently, her cheeks warming.

"He doesn't know you once lived in San Francisco? That you worked there?"

"Somehow the subject has never arisen."

That was the truth, Elly realized as she hung up the phone. Jess had only seen her in her small-town setting. He'd assumed she'd always lived on the coast and hadn't seemed interested in hearing too much about her past. Since Elly no longer had any real interest in her own past, that arrangement had suited her fine. Besides, she had sensed that Jess had liked her the way she was. She fit his inner concept of the kind of wife he wanted. There had been no point in telling him that she'd once lived quite a different life-style. She had been cautious about jeopardizing his image of her.

But his comment regarding her feeling underdressed in San Francisco was really too much. If Jess Winter was going to find out just what Aunt Clara and the family were like this weekend, he might as well learn that there was another side to Elly Trent, as well.

Elly stayed by herself in a Portland hotel on Friday evening. She wanted time to assess the purchases she had made that day and play with makeup. She hadn't delved into blushers and eye shadow for quite a while. The tiny Italian shoes were going to hurt her feet, but she vowed to ignore the pain. She would be back into moccasins on

Tuesday. Recreating the elegant chignon she used to wear when she worked in San Francisco took a little practice, but eventually she was satisfied with the results. The peach silk blouse, narrow white wool skirt and soft peach jacket were nothing short of perfect. She hardly recognized herself.

On Saturday morning Elly put the whole look together, examined herself in front of a mirror and declared herself satisfied. She looked very "Big City." She drove to the address Jess had given her with a sense of grim anticipation. Whatever else happened this weekend he was going to learn that he didn't know everything there was to know about Elly Trent.

It wasn't until she stood in the hallway of Jess's expensive apartment building that Elly had a few second thoughts. Hesitantly, she raised her hand and then, telling herself it was too late to change her mind, she knocked. The door was opened almost immediately, and Jess stood staring down at her. He was dressed to express quiet corporate power, from his gray vested suite to his subdued silk tie. She found herself staring back. Neither one of them commented on the other's attire.

"Am I on time?" Elly asked sweetly, glancing around the sophisticated living room.

"Yes." He shut the door and stood with his hands behind him on the knob. Jess watched her survey the room. "You're on time."

"I didn't want to interfere with your schedule." She swung around, smiling brilliantly.

"I rarely let anyone interfere with my schedule. Let me grab my flight bag and I'll be ready to go." He walked past her, heading for the bedroom.

Elly experienced a moment of trepidation as she heard the coolness in his voice. This wasn't quite what she had expected. On the other hand, she hadn't been certain exactly how he would react to the "other" Elly Trent.

He hadn't even kissed her hello.

"Where's your suitcase?" he asked as he returned.

"Downstairs in my car."

He nodded. "We'll put your car in my slot in the garage. We can take the Jag to the airport." With calm efficiency he went around turning out lights, picked up a file folder lying on an end table and then he held the door for Elly.

Slightly bemused by his attitude, Elly stepped meekly out into the hall. Wasn't he going to say anything at all about the way she looked? She waited for some comment all the way to the airport.

"I don't know if I ever mentioned it or not, but I used to work in San Francisco," she said later when they were strapped into their seats aboard the southbound jet.

Jess glanced up from the papers he had removed from the folder. "Did you?" He didn't seem particularly interested.

"I had a job with a large corporation. I was working my way up through management when I decided that wasn't what I wanted to do for the rest of my life." God help her; she was starting to babble. Why was she telling him all this? He hadn't asked. She had wanted him to ask.

"I had no idea." He went back to the file he was studying.

"Well, I didn't just spring into existence at the age of thirty behind my cash register."

"Apparently not."

Elly gave up. Subsiding into a thoughtful silence, she accepted a glass of juice from the flight attendant and contemplated the seat in front of her. Damn it, she could be aloof and cool, too. That attitude went with her clothes and hairstyle, didn't it?

It wasn't until she walked into the hotel room that afternoon and took in the significance of the double bed that Elly began to have a few doubts about her own ability to maintain the arrogant, feminine facade. Of course Jess would expect her to stay in the same room with him. After Wednesday night he had no reason to think otherwise. If she admitted the truth to herself, she couldn't deny that was the way she wanted things, too. But she felt strangely unsettled. The only solution she could discover was to retreat further and further into her sophisticated, cool image.

"When's your meeting with Harrigan?" She stood in front of the mirror, tucking wayward tendrils of hair back into a chignon. She watched Jess as he crossed the room to pick up the phone.

"In an hour. I'm going to call him now and let him know I'll be on time."

"You mean that *we'll* be on time." Elly turned to confront him, frowning faintly. "I'm going to this meeting, too, Jess."

"There's no need for you to be there."

His casual dismissal of her role in the proceedings almost took her breath away. "May I remind you, Jess Winter, that I am the major stockholder of Trentco? If I may be blunt about it, Harrigan works for me. And as long as you're playing financial consultant, you damn well work for me, too! I'm going to attend that meeting between the two of you. Do I make myself clear?"

He glanced at her as he dialed Harrigan's number. One brow rose consideringly. "Very clear, *boss*. You must have been hell to work for back in the the days when you were climbing up through the management ranks."

Elly felt as if he'd slapped her. She watched, shocked, as he spoke to Matt Harrigan. *Hell to work for.* Was that how he saw her in her new clothes and elegant hairstyle? She had wanted to appear sophisticated and dynamic. But perhaps she was coming across as cold and hard-edged. He had described his ex-wife that way. Belatedly Elly recalled that when Jess had met Marina she had been an executive in a large corporation.

Perhaps she was beginning to remind him of Marina Carrington.

Quite suddenly, Elly saw her attempt to impress Jess in a whole new light. What if everything she had done today had only served to make him think of Marina? Elly could have wept in sheer frustration. She began to feel trapped by the image she had created. On top of that she didn't know how to breach the barrier that seemed to be between herself and Jess today. She thought of the rather daring, off-the-shoulder black silk dress she had bought to wear that evening and shuddered. She was very much afraid it would make her look like a very expensively attired witch.

Resentment picked her nerves, making her feel restless and defiant. She had a right to dress the way she wanted. If she were to marry Jess she would continue to dress this way on the occasions when they traveled. Damn it, she couldn't go through her whole life terrified of saying or doing something that reminded him of Marina. She was an individual in her own right with all the corresponding rights and privileges.

"Four-thirty will be fine. We'll meet you downstairs in the lobby." Jess paused, flicking a glance at Elly's warning expression. "Yes, Elly's coming along, too. Says she wants to be there. Pointed out that all things considered, she's the boss."

Elly could hear the faint sound of Harrigan's laughter on the other end of the line. He said something that made Jess grin reluctantly before he replaced the phone. He stood with his hands on his hips, feet slightly apart and regarded Elly thoughtfully.

"Harrigan says you're the one who hired him."

Elly lifted her chin, daring him to criticize. "He seemed like the right man for the job. I had to make a decision when my uncle died, Jess. The family was at each other's throats, bickering constantly about the fate of the company. No one was doing anything constructive for Trentco. I, ah, came down to San Francisco and made what I guess you'd call an executive decision. I put Harrigan in charge and went back home."

"How did you know him in the first place?"

"He'd been working for my uncle. I knew Uncle Toby trusted him and had been more or less grooming him to take over the responsibility of running Trentco."

"You authorized one hell of an incentive package for Harrigan, apparently. Good salary, bonuses, a lot of decision-making power."

Elly couldn't tell if Jess was criticizing her or not. "It seemed like the right thing to do at the time. I have faith in Harrigan, and I'd like to give him a chance to revive Trentco. There are a lot of people's jobs at stake, Jess. People who worked for my uncle for years and who were fiercely loyal. A lot of them would go if the company were bought out. It seems wrong to sell off a company that's been in the family for so many years. I know my aunt and a lot of the others are only thinking of the immediate profit, but there's another generation coming along. Kids like my cousin Dave. In a sense, Trentco is part of their heritage. Someday one of them may want to take a crack at running it."

"It comes down to the fact that you don't want to sell."

"Exactly." She wondered if he were going to advise her otherwise. "My uncle left me the controlling portion of shares because, even though he knew I didn't particularly want to run the firm, I'd keep it safe for the next generation. It's a responsibility I can't just walk away from, Jess."

"I know."

She relaxed a little. "I'm glad you understand."

"Let's go meet Harrigan."

Matthew Harrigan was in his early thirties, an intelligent, aggressive man who could also be quite charming when he chose. He was dark-eyed, attractive and recently married. Elly was a little disappointed that his wife hadn't accompanied him. She said as much as she introduced him to Jess.

Harrigan chuckled. "Diane said she preferred to stay clear of the screaming match. I guess she thought your aunt and uncle and some of the others were going to be here."

"The screaming match comes later," Elly said. "Jess has invited them all to dinner."

Harrigan regarded the older man with blatant admiration. "Brave man."

"Are they that bad?" Jess led the way into the quiet atmosphere of the hotel lounge and seated Elly.

Harrigan eyed him thoughtfully. "I think you'll be able to handle them. Elly does it the easy way by putting a lot of distance between herself and them." He smiled at Elly. "A policy her Uncle Toby would have understood even if he would have been disappointed."

Jess's eyes narrowed. "Disappointed?"

"Didn't you know? Toby Trent had always hoped Elly would assume control of Trentco. He claimed she was the only one in the family who had a head for business. Elly very gently tried to tell him she didn't think she wanted the job, but Toby was as stubborn as everyone else in the family. He figured if he left the shares to her she wouldn't have any choice."

Cool curiosity dawned in Jess's eyes as he glanced at Elly, who was concentrating on the glass of Napa Valley chardonnay she'd ordered. "But Elly went ahead with her own plans?"

Harrigan grinned, either unaware or choosing to ignore the tension at the table. "Elly had already made her decision. Toby figured the move to the coast was merely a passing fancy that she would outgrow. He figured she'd return after his death."

"But she didn't."

"She came back long enough to put me in charge, an act for which the rest of the family isn't prepared to forgive her." Harrigan's eyes lit up as he broke into laughter.

"Perhaps," Jess said coolly, "they'll change their minds this evening."

Elly winced at his unruffled confidence. Jess simply didn't know what he was going to be facing.

But Elly did have an idea of what she was going to be up against, and in the end she dressed to meet the challenge. There was no point reverting to her casual seaside look. The damage had probably already been done, as far as Jess was concerned. She might as well finish off the evening the way she had started the day. Feeling as if she were writing her own unhappy ending, she disappeared into the hotel bathroom shortly before dinner to dress.

When she had bought the coolly elegant yet undeniably sensuous silk, she had imagined overwhelming Jess with the impact. Now she slipped into it feeling as if she were dressing for battle. She knew she had become quieter and quieter during the afternoon. So had Jess. The result had been an almost complete cessation of communication. Elly didn't want to think about what would happen when they eventually returned to the room that evening. How did you go to bed with someone with whom you weren't on speaking terms?

Jess took one look at the distant, serenely aloof vision that appeared from the bathroom and nodded once. His eyes gave no indication of what he was thinking, but Elly shivered as she saw the ice in them. She began to panic about what would happen later.

"Ready?" he asked, making a final adjustment to his tie in the mirror.

"Yes." At his lack of response to her elegant armor, Elly retreated even further behind it. Her sole goal in life focused on a grim determination just to get through the evening.

Jess's expression darkened, but he said nothing. He merely reached for his keys and opened the door for her.

The ring of stubborn, hostile Trent faces waiting downstairs in the lobby of the hotel was enough to make Elly feel even grimmer than she already did. As she always did on those rare occasions when she was pushed into a corner from which there was no escape, she fought back with a kind of grim determination. She was a Trent, too, and there were times when she could be just as stubborn as the rest. This time the war was waged with cool hauteur and almost savagely polite manners. Challengingly she made introductions.

Aunt Clara stepped forward first, a battleship moving into combat. She examined Jess with a critical eye. She was dressed in the customary knit suit that sheathed her elderly figure. Her gray hair was pinned into a severe bun, and her eyes sparkled with the prospect of battle.

"I do hope you will listen to reason, Mr. Winter, since Elly obviously will not."

"I always listen to reason," Jess murmured and then proceeded to dispense his most charming smile. "Especially when it's all in the family."

To Elly's surprise, Aunt Clara blinked under the impact of the smile and then stepped back to introduce her husband and the remainder of the small landing party. She had brought only the most formidable members of the clan with her tonight, Elly observed as she went through the ritual of introductions. In order, she greeted Clara's husband, Uncle Frank, who always backed his wife's judgments; Aunt Alice and Uncle Jim, who had their eyes on a yacht that they hoped to buy with the profits from Trentco's sale; and cousin Cathy, who had no interest in business and even less in thinking of the future. She had just been through a divorce and was bent on restructuring her social life. Cathy was a likable woman, but she tended to live very much in the present. Her two young children were part of the reason why Elly wanted the family to hold on to the company. If it were sold tomorrow, Cathy would have the profits spent by next Thursday. There was no malice in Cathy, but it simply wouldn't occur to her to sock the money away for the children's education.

"How did you get involved in all this?" Frank Gaines inquired aggressively of Jess as the crowd was seated in a corner of the hotel's dining room.

"Isn't it obvious? I'm about to become part of the family. It's only natural Elly would ask for some advice."

Elly's eyes widened at the blatant lie. She had never asked him for advice. In fact she'd been doing her utmost to keep Jess out of this.

Aunt Clara was already pouncing. "Part of the family? What's that supposed to mean? Just because you're living with her on a casual basis doesn't mean you're *family*!"

"Elly and I will be married next month." Placidly, Jess opened his menu while everyone else at the table absorbed the news.

It was Cathy who recovered first and turned to Elly in amazement. "You're marrying him? He doesn't look at all like the sort of man I thought you'd end up with. I thought you were dating various and assorted bearded dropouts."

"The wedding," Elly tried to say firmly, "hasn't been actually scheduled yet."

Jess glanced up from the menu. "The wedding," he said just as firmly, "is very much on schedule."

Elly didn't know how to respond so she took refuge once more behind her barricade of silk and makeup.

From that position, she watched Jess calmly take control of the evening. He listened until Aunt Clara ran out of breath and arguments, and then he put forth his own rationale for not selling Trentco. To Elly's astonishment, everyone paid attention.

Not only did they pay attention, but as the dessert arrived there was even a gathering sense of agreement around the table. Jess's assurance and obvious expertise were proving persuasive. He never once lost his temper and he was extraordinarily patient. But he had an instinct for using the right approach on each individual at the table.

"Cathy. Elly tells me you have two young children. I realize you probably think that taking the immediate profit and putting it in the bank for the kids' education is the safest move, but in the long run there will be more economic security in this if Trentco is revived."

"Well, I..." Cathy stammered, unable to explain that she really hasn't been thinking that far ahead.

"I know you're a good mother and want to do what's best for the children," Jess went on easily. "Believe me, this is your best option.

"Now about that boat you're thinking of buying, Jim. I think we can arrange some kind of loan against your stock. Something just between you and me. Believe me, after looking at the Trentco financial picture, I have no objection to your using your shares as collateral. Wouldn't mind owning some in the least. That way you'll have the best of both worlds.

"Clara, we're talking family tradition here. I seriously doubt that you'd want to sell off the Trent family heritage. You're the kind of woman who values the important things in life, the meaningful things. It's people of your generation who have to protect family heritages, don't you agree? I want you to take another look at this."

It went like that for some time, with Jess managing to find just the right button to push with each member of the family. By the time everyone rose to leave, Elly was mesmerized by the adept way Jess had handled the entire evening. Monday's vote had become a mere formality. The family was now in agreement. Aunt Clara paused in the lobby to pat Elly's hand.

"You're a lucky young woman, my dear. You've always had such an unruly streak of independence in you that we couldn't help but worry on occasion. Now I think you're in good hands. Good night, Elly." She beamed at Jess, who was standing beside Elly. "See you both on Monday."

Uncle Jim pumped Jess's hand. "Did you mean what you said about that loan?"

"I always mean what I say," Jess assured him.

"Great! That's wonderful. I'll get in touch with you later." He grinned at Elly. "Elly doesn't understand how badly I've wanted a seagoing boat. She hates the sea, you know. Or, at least, she hates swimming in it. It's scared her ever since that time when she was a teenager. She was at the beach with my boy, Dave, who was just a little tyke, then. He got out too far and got himself into trouble. Elly swam out to get him. Brave kid. The water was rough, and some fool watching on shore thought he saw a shark. You can imagine the panic. But Elly here just kept swimming, dragging little Dave back with her. Gave us all one hell of a scare. Elly's stayed out of the sea ever since."

"Elly can be very determined about some things," Jess murmured with a sidelong glance at her. "Good night, Jim. I'm glad to have met you."

The other man nodded pleasantly and turned to join the others.

Elly stood very still in the center of the plush lobby, unaware of the well-dressed people coming and going around her. She stared after the last of the family.

"Very impressive, Jess," she said at last.

"I told you they weren't going to be all that tough, Elly." He took her arm and guided her toward the elevators.

"But it won't be the end of it, Jess," she said desperately. "Don't you understand? Aunt Clara will start calling on you constantly for advice. And what was all that about a loan to Uncle Jim? And Cathy's going to expect you to take a lasting interest in her two kids now. Jess, don't you see? You're getting yourself involved in a very messy family situation!''

"I can handle it." He seemed totally unconcerned. In the hall outside their room he paused to get out his key. "They're all easy to figure out. You're the tough one, Elly." He opened the door.

She glanced up at him warily as she walked inside.

"What do you mean, I'm the tough one?"

He shut the door and turned to study her. "I think you know." His eyes moved over the cool, expensive facade she had created for herself. He folded his arms and leaned back against the door.

The sensation of being pushed into a corner intensified. Elly stared at him, torn between uncertainty, resentment and fear. Instead of coming out of the corner fighting this time, she frantically began to explain.

"It was all because you implied I wouldn't have the right clothes for the city. I was upset because you kept insisting on getting involved with this messy business. I decided to show you that I wasn't just a...a hick who had only jeans in her closet. Jess, it's very complicated to explain, but I guess I wanted you to see there was another side to me. I never thought...never realized..."

Jess came purposefully away from the door. "Any more surprises in store?"

She shook her head forlornly. "No."

"Good. I think I've had about enough today. I'm ready for the real Elly." He came to a halt in front of her and threaded his hands through her carefully contrived chignon. Quite deliberately he pulled her chestnut hair free and watched in satisfaction as it tumbled around her shoulders.

"You're not angry?" she asked hesitantly.

"Still love me?" he countered.

She threw herself into his arms, wrapping him fiercely around the waist. "Of course I still love you."

"Then I'm not angry." His voice darkened with the first stirrings of desire as his hands went to the thin zipper at the back of her gown.

Seven

A long time later Jess quietly contemplated the hotel room ceiling and the sense of relaxation that pervaded his body. He was cradling Elly in one arm. She seemed to be asleep and that pleased him somehow. She looked so trusting, so *right*—a woman who had just surrendered to her lover and who now bore the subtle evidence of his claim on every inch of her body. Jess's claim. When she was lying like this, limp and still damp from his love-making, he felt so much more certain of her.

Lately it seemed as if he'd been engaged in some sort of unnamed warfare, the rules of which were being set by Elly. She was both his opponent and the prize of victory. For the past two months everything had been proceeding on schedule. The shift in his life-style was going according to plan. Elly had seemed to fit into that plan so perfectly that Jess couldn't believe she didn't see it for herself.

But there was no doubt about the fact that things had been going wrong ever since Carrington had pulled that Peeping Tom stunt. Damn the man. He had always been a source of malicious mischief. Jess had been so sure the guy was out of his life for good. Why the hell did he have to choose now to reappear? This time, Jess vowed, he would have to do something permanent about Carrington. That threat on Wednesday evening was the last straw. There were ways of dealing with men such as Carrington. Jess decided he would find one. The man was a born con artist. He couldn't have lived this long without having broken a few laws involving fraud or misrepresentation. Perhaps the research that the investigation firm was doing would turn up enough to throw the fear of jail into him. If that didn't work Jess had no qualms now about taking more drastic steps.

Carrington had come near Elly. Any closer and, as far as Jess was concerned, the other man had written his own sentence. No one would really miss Damon Carrington.

But some damage had been done, there was no doubt about it. Elly had begun questioning the relationship and all the plans Jess had spent so much time making. She had begun withdrawing, as if she were trying to put an emotional distance between herself and him. She had tried to keep him out of the private side of her life. And this morning, when she'd arrived on his doorstep looking so coolly formal and aloof, he'd known just how far things had gone.

It was a battle, all right. He'd had to force his way into her family business. She should have welcomed his advice and expertise. She should have wanted to share the problems with him. Instead, he'd been obliged to push past her defenses and assume the role of her consultant.

It wasn't, Jess decided objectively, that he had any real doubts about winning the war. The little barricades Elly tried to maintain were fundamentally undermined by the fact that she loved him. Still, it annoyed him that he had to fight in the first place. She should have accepted the situation for what it was. Jess was considering that when she stirred in his arms.

"Jess?"

"Hmm?" He tightened his arm around her and rolled onto his side to look down into her face. The shadows of the room concealed the color of her eyes, but he thought he could detect some of the warmth of the gold in them.

"I wasn't sure if you were awake," she murmured.

"I don't dare go to sleep while you're lying on my arm. It would be numb by morning."

"Oh! I'm sorry, I didn't realize." She started to struggle but he gently pushed her back.

"Don't worry about it. I'll let you know when the circulation problem gets critical." He dipped his head and kissed away a trace of dampness between her breasts. The scent of her filled his mind and his body. It was a warm, earthy, utterly feminine fragrance, and he realized vaguely that he was incredibly attracted by it. It was uniquely Elly and he would know it anywhere. The human male was a very primitive animal in many respects. "You smell so good."

"Very gallant. The truth is I probably smell the way I do after I've spent a day stocking shelves and hauling out old produce." She touched his shoulder experimentally, drawing a small pattern on his skin.

Jess turned his head to kiss her wrist. "You smell sexy and very female. I like it."

"Beast."

"I was just thinking the same thing." He met her eyes again, the small smile that had been edging his mouth disappearing. "Elly?"

"Umm?"

"I want you to tell me you're finished playing stubborn little games as far as your family business problems are concerned." He felt her stiffen slightly under the weight of his sprawled body, but he made no move to ease away from her. Damn it, Jess thought, he wanted her to know she couldn't keep trying to dodge him on this issue.

"I'm not playing games, Jess."

"You've been trying to keep me at arm's length ever since Carrington showed up at your window the night you set out to seduce me. You wanted time. You didn't want me getting involved, you said. You started backing away, started acting warily. Don't pretend otherwise, Elly. Everything was going fine up until that point. You knew we were going to get married, and you weren't questioning it or anything else."

She stared up at him. "That's not quite true, Jess. I was having a few qualms. And after you thought you saw your ex-wife at the window, I had a lot more!"

"After seeing Carrington you must realize I wasn't having visions that night!"

She nodded uneasily. "I realize that. You've told me they were twins, and I suppose a brief glimpse of his face at the window would be enough to startle you into thinking you'd seen her face."

"Since there's a logical explanation for what I admit wasn't exactly the most diplomatic thing I've ever done, why the continued wariness? Why try to keep me at bay?"

She braced her hands against his chest as if trying to keep him from holding her closer. The action irritated him. Deliberately, Jess leaned more heavily along the length of her.

"I told you, Jess, I'd been a little uncertain about our relationship before that night. Afterward, I started doing some serious thinking."

"You mean you started getting nervous," he corrected bluntly.

"Well, yes, I did."

"Even though you know damn well you're in love with me." Her lashes lowered, veiling her gaze. She didn't respond to the statement, but Jess sensed the stubborn resistance in her and was determined to break it. He leaned forward and brushed his mouth lightly over hers. "Say it, Elly," he murmured. "Tell me again that you love me."

She surrendered on a small sigh. "I love you, Jess. But that doesn't mean I'm going to marry you."

"You will," he said. "I guarantee it."

"I have to be sure, Jess," she whispered pleadingly.

"Of what? That I want you? You've got proof of that by now, and I'll be happy to supply more. Sure of the fact that I'll look out for your best interests? I've shown you I'll do that, too, even though I have to get past your roadblocks in order to accomplish that goal. Sure that we're compatible? We've spent enough time together for you to know that by now, too. Elly, for over two months you've known where we were headed. What's more, you've come along very willingly until recently. There's no need to get stubborn and defensive now. You're in love with me, and you're going to marry me. That's final."

"It is not final," she said, her temper flaring. "I'd like to be sure of a few other things, too!"

"Such as?" He caught her wrists and pinned them to the pillow beside her head.

"For starters, I'd like to be sure I won't have to spend the rest of my life walking on eggs, worrying about saying or doing something that reminds you of your past."

He was startled. "Reminds me of my past? What in hell are you talking about?"

Her eyes turned mutinous. "I saw your face when you opened the door this morning. You took one look at me and went cold. You've been acting that way all day. It was because I reminded you of Marina, wasn't it? That was probably the way she used to dress. All you've ever seen me in is jeans. Then you found out I used to work in the business world the way she did. I haven't spent my whole life in a small town on the coast. I used to be very 'Big City,' too. Just like she was."

He glared at her for a minute and then groaned as he realized what was going through her head. "Listen to me, Elly Trent, you couldn't remind me of Marina Carrington if you tried. The difference between the two of you is like night and day."

"Then why were you so . . . so distant all day?"

"Because I thought you had deliberately used the clothes and the hairstyle and the makeup as another way of keeping me at arm's length," he said growled. "It was as if you were trying to wear a sign that said Don't Touch. If you want the truth, it made me angry. It sure as hell didn't remind me of Marina. What made you think you could hide the real Elly beneath the stylish clothes and the big-city manner? Or that I'd ever mistake you for someone else?"

Looking up at him, Elly suddenly realized he was telling the truth. No man could look that impatient and that thoroughly annoyed unless he was genuinely irked at her misunderstanding. She began to feel a little foolish. "Well, it was a logical assumption for me to make. It was the only reason I could think of for your actions today."

"It was not a logical assumption. It was a damn stupid assumption. Now that we've disposed of that notion, let's talk about something else. Why have you been trying to keep me out of your family business problems? You've been digging in your sweet heels every step of the way. I'd like a good reason."

She gazed up at him mutely for an instant. Then Elly said carefully, "I've told you, Jess. I didn't want you getting involved."

"That's not good enough. I want to know why."

Elly lost her own patience. "Because I was afraid that would remind you of the past, too. You'd told me about all the family financial problems you'd had with the Carringtons. I was terrified you'd start equating my family business problems with them. I was afraid you'd see us all as leeches."

His gray eyes gleamed with sudden fierceness. "Of all the dumb, idiotic, crazy ideas. Elly, that's nonsense. There's nothing remotely similar about the two situations. There couldn't be. Don't you understand that? You're you. Nothing connected with you could be in any way the same as it was with the Carringtons. Believe me, it's inconceivable."

"Jess, are you sure?" She searched his face, seeking confirmation.

"Of course I'm sure. Damn sure! And I think you know it. You're just using this as a smoke screen, aren't you? An excuse to take your time making up your mind about whether or not to marry me.''

''That's not true!''

''Good,'' he said forcefully, ''because it's not going to work. I've put up with your shadow dancing long enough, Elly. You and I are getting married. Next month, just as I told your relatives. I'm not giving you any more rope, lady, or you'll manage to get both of us snarled in it.''

''Please, Jess, be reasonable. We can't just rush into marriage because you've established a timetable for it. You've got to see that there are too many things we don't yet know about each other. We need time.''

''What don't we know about each other?'' he challenged.

''Well, take my past, for instance. You didn't know anything about it before today. You never even asked about it.''

''It wasn't exactly a crucial topic as far as I was concerned.''

''Because the way I am, my life-style on the coast seemed to fit so perfectly into all your plans and requirements,'' she shot back. ''That's all you saw and that's all you cared about.''

For a moment frustrated anger burned in his eyes, and his hands tightened on her wrists. Elly wished she didn't feel so terribly vulnerable.

''It wasn't all I cared about, but it seemed to be all that was important at the time. It's still all that's important. But if it makes you feel any better, tell me about your past. What made you decide to leave San Francisco and the business world?''

''This is hardly the time to go into that,'' she protested.

"Seems like the perfect time to me. The fact that I haven't asked until now appears to be another road-block you're throwing out. So, okay, I'm asking."

"I don't get the feeling you're really interested."

Jess smiled faintly. He used the pad of his thumb on the inside of her wrist. "You're wrong there, Elly. Everything about you interests me. The subject of your past is now on the table and open for discussion. Talk."

"All right, I'll keep it short and simple so as not to bore you. I realized three years ago that big-city business and big-city living wasn't something I wanted on a full-time basis. When I began to understand that, I began to change my life. At the time it was easy enough. My family was upset, but basically there wasn't anything they could do. I decided I wasn't obliged to live my life to suit them. Unfortunately, Uncle Toby made up his mind I wasn't going to be allowed to escape so easily. He always said I was the only adult member of the clan who had a head for business and a sense of responsibility."

"So he left controlling interest in Trentco to you. You're in charge until the next generation comes along. In a sense the company still ties you to your old life."

"You've got it."

"That's all there is to it? No tragic love affairs? No failed marriage? No flickering fires of passion that never had a chance to run their course?"

"No! Damn it, stop teasing me, Jess. I was running toward something, not away from it. It was an intellectual decision as well as an emotional one."

"Elly, my sweet, this may come as a shock to you, but your lurid past isn't exactly a big surprise."

"It isn't?"

"Honey, I've seen your wine collection, your tape collection and your book collection. I've seen the skill with which you run your business and the way you keep accounts. I've seen the way you use gourmet cooking techniques to make things like sprouts and lentils into fine cuisine. If I'd worried about it, it wouldn't have been hard to guess that you spent a few years somewhere else besides a tiny town on the coast."

"Oh."

"You made a decision, the same kind of decision I made," he concluded blandly.

She looked at him suspiciously, "What's that supposed to mean?"

His expression softened. The element of indulgent amusement that she was accustomed to seeing in his eyes was back. "Just that you and I have one more thing in common now. We both chose to leave the world of big business for another kind of life-style. Does that give you a little more reassurance? Because that's what you're looking for, isn't it?"

"Perhaps." A flicker of resentment went through her. She wouldn't need all this reassurance, she realized, if she just knew that Jess loved her. "Can you blame me for being uncertain, Jess?"

"Yes," he said unhesitatingly. "You've had time enough to get to know me. You shouldn't still be questioning my actions or my motives. Furthermore, you ought to have a little more faith in my ability to think for myself. I can tell the difference between the past and the present, and I sure as hell know the difference between you and Marina Carrington."

Elly nodded, feeling chastened. "I believe you."

"Fine. Then believe me when I tell you we're going to be married next month, and there's not a thing you can do about it except show up on time."

"I don't think you even realize just how arrogant you are."

"I realize it, all right. But I'm running out of patience."

"You mean your schedule is starting to slip, and you don't like to have your plans upset," she told him bluntly. "I, on the other hand, don't take too well to being programmed. One of the reasons I decided to leave corporate life is that I don't like being on someone else's schedule. It's too much like being on a menu. There's a fair-sized chance of being chewed up and swallowed."

Jess considered her for a long moment. "Are you by any chance afraid of me, Elly, honey?"

"No, I am not!"

"Still love me?" His fingertips on her wrists began to move in wider circles. His gray eyes were taunting. He knew the answer.

Flustered, Elly sighed in exasperation. She felt trapped. "Yes, I still love you, but that doesn't mean I'm going to marry you next month!"

He lowered his head and lingeringly kissed her throat. "You're the only woman who has ever told me she loved me and meant it. Do you have any idea of how much that means to me? I'd walk through hell for your kind of love. Pacifying a few relatives for you is nothing."

"Oh, Jess..." She felt herself weakening almost at once. She was so very vulnerable to him, Elly thought in despair.

"We both know you're going to marry me, sweetheart." His mouth glided gently over the tip of her breast, and Elly shivered faintly. "I want your love. I want all the softness in you as well as the fire. I need to know you belong to me."

"And in return, Jess?" Her fingers trembled as her palm flattened on his shoulder. "What will you give me in return?

"Everything that counts. Everything I have to give a woman."

"I want to be loved, Jess. Do you think you'll ever be able to give me that?"

He went still, lifting his head to meet her pleading gaze. "Elly," he said slowly, "I don't know. I'm not sure I ever really knew what it meant to love in the first place. I said I'll give you all I have to give. That's as much as I can promise."

"You seem willing enough to take my love."

He framed her face with his hands and smiled down at her. "That's because your love is so beautifully easy to recognize for what it is. It's very clear, very soft, very real. I know you love me. My own feelings are too complex for me to sort out right now. But they're real, too. Elly, I want you so badly I can taste it. Maybe that's love. Do you want me to use the words?"

She put her fingertips against his mouth. "No, not unless you know what you're talking about. Not unless you mean them. I think you're the one who's afraid, Jess."

"Afraid of what?" His eyes lost some of their indulgent warmth.

"Of surrendering to love. It's easy enough to let someone love you. After all, there's no risk involved. But it's far more reckless to be the one who loves. I think you've become a cautious man over the years. Perhaps Marina Carrington made you that way. Or perhaps you were always that way. It doesn't really matter now. What does matter is that you feel safer when your life is very firmly under control and on schedule. Having me love you fits in very nicely with your plans. But loving me in return would entail some unknowns, wouldn't it? You'd have to take a few risks. You'd have to make yourself vulnerable. I'm sure you find it much safer to stay on top of the situation emotionally. This way you think you have it all."

"I think," Jess said coolly, "that's about enough of the amateur psychoanalysis. I like it better when you're making love to me, not discussing it."

"You'll have to excuse me," she snapped. "Maybe all this sex is rotting my brain."

"The problem," Jess informed her as he slipped boldly into the cradle of her thighs, "is that you haven't had nearly enough yet to set your thinking straight. But I'll be happy to work on the problem."

"Jess, this is no way to settle an argument! We should talk this out.... Ah, *Jess*." His name was a husky sound of capitulation. He was there between her thighs, probing the soft folds of her feminity, testing for a renewed response. In spite of herself, Elly knew her body was already giving him what he demanded.

She could feel herself growing moist and sensitized, knew Jess was taking blatant satisfaction in the reaction he was provoking. He nestled his head beside her on the pillow and began whispering heavy, dark, infinitely arousing words of passion and promise. All the while he teased her with his body. The slow entrance was followed by a tantalizing withdrawal. Over and over again Jess played on the pattern until Elly thought she would go out of her mind.

Finally, in gathering desperation, she pushed at him. He fell back obediently, and she slithered astride his hips. Closing her eyes she lowered herself, taking her fill at last. She moaned in soft pleasure as she took him inside her.

When Elly lifted her lashes, she found Jess laughing up at her with his eyes, the triumphant male.

"You are a beast," she told him and ran her fingers upward through the curly hair of his chest. Slowly, she leaned forward until her breasts were pressed against him.

"So are you, sweetheart. A very sweet lady beast who's been running free a little too long. But I know how to tame you."

"Think so?" She felt good up here on top of him, Elly decided. She felt in command for once.

"Watch this," he ordered, his voice thick with promise. "I'll have you eating out of the palm of my hand in no time."

Slowly, he began to move inside her. His hands went to her hips, holding her in place while he established the cadence he wanted. Elly shuddered and gripped his shoulders, seeking to quicken the pace. She felt the tension began to coil inside her and became more assertive as she sought its release. This kind of excitement was still new to her. It was associated with only one man, and she knew in her heart it would always be that way.

"Jess, you're deliberately tormenting me."

"It's nice work if you can get it. And I've got it."

Her nails sank warningly into his shoulders when he refused to pick up the pace beneath her. Jess ignored the small punishment. The slow entrance and withdrawal pattern continued, and even though she was on top of him Elly found herself helpless to alter it. The frustratingly slow rhythm seemed to be setting fire to all her senses. She tried to wriggle a bit and found herself anchored by Jess's large, strong hands.

"Tell me you love me, Elly."

"What will you give me if I do?"

"What you're looking for."

"Promise?" she breathed.

"My word of honor."

Voice aching with passion and love, Elly whispered, "I love you, Jess."

"Don't ever stop telling me, Elly."

His fingers slipped around her thighs to cup her buttocks, and he began to move with fierce power. Elly cried out softly as the sensation in her lower body became unbearable. The inevitable release sent spasms of excitement through her, leaving her shivering and voiceless for a long moment.

Jess felt the pulsating response and was drawn by it into his own shuddering satisfaction. He gripped Elly with all his strength, driving up into her until both of them gave way beneath the overwhelming onslaught.

"I love you, Jess."

The words were mere threads of sound as Elly collapsed in a damp, sensual sprawl.

"Elly, my sweet, sexy, lovely Elly..." Jess held her close, making no effort to separate their still-fused bodies. This time he went right to sleep without spending any time contemplating the ceiling or the future.

On Tuesday evening Elly wandered through her house watering plants and dusting various surfaces with a preoccupied air. Jess had phoned a few minutes earlier to make certain she had arrived safely from Portland. He had sounded satisfied with himself in more ways than one, and she knew he thought he had everything, including her, under control.

"We're back on schedule," she told the African violets in the kitchen window. "On time and on line. Trentco has been saved for the next generation, some semblance of family ties has been restored, and yours truly has been brought to heel. Leave it to an expert to get things back in order. I suppose I should be grateful he's not charging his usual fees."

She could hardly complain about the way Jess had handled the family situation, Elly told herself. The man had done exactly what he'd said he would do. He'd convinced everyone, including Aunt Clara, that he knew what he was doing, and they had all obediently voted not to sell Trentco. Matt Harrigan was delighted and promised immediate signs of increased profits. Order had been brought out of chaos and discord.

Elly had been forced to realize that she had been fretting over nothing. Jess hadn't associated her short-lived stylishness with his ex-wife. He'd simply been annoyed because he had assumed Elly was trying to maintain a certain distance. Nor had he been even slightly ruffled by the effort it took to deal with her squabbling relatives. Apparently after dealing with the Carringtons, the Trents seemed quite tame to him. Again she had worried for no good reason.

Elly wandered into the living room and stood glaring thoughtfully at the collection of ivy plants. She'd done a lot of worrying lately. In fact, it amounted to more than worrying, and it was all connected to Jess Winter. She'd accused him of being afraid to love, but when she viewed the matter objectively, she could see that she was the one who had spent so much time being afraid lately.

She'd been afraid of pushing him, afraid of provoking a violent confrontation between Jess and Damon Carrington, afraid of reminding Jess of his ex-wife, afraid that her own family troubles might be equated with the problems he'd had with the Carringtons.

Good grief, Elly thought as she tipped the watering can over the ivy plant, *I'm the one who's been running scared.* She had let her love of Jess make her a nervous wreck.

Alarmed by the sudden direction of her reasoning, Elly continued through the house with the watering can. By the time she arrived back in the living room she was deep in thought. Absently, she gazed at herself in the mirror that hung over the fireplace. Her intently frowning image gazed back at her.

She was formulating a lecture, one she intended to administer to herself, when another face materialized in the mirror. Through the open drapes of the window behind her a woman was watching her—a stunningly beautiful woman with long blond hair.

Elly knew before she whirled around that even though she couldn't see the woman's eyes clearly, they would be a vivid green.

"Marina!"

Eight

Shock held Elly immobilized for several endless seconds after the woman's face had disappeared. If that was the mysterious prowler Jess had seen the night she had tried to seduce him, it was no wonder he had muttered his ex-wife's name. Elly went cold as she stood staring at the window. Damon in a wig? A woman made up to resemble Marina Carrington? And for God's sake, *why*? Whoever it was had been laughing at her.

It was that fact that finally gave Elly the impetus to lurch away from the front of the mirror. Without pausing to think, she hurled herself across the room and yanked open the front door.

She found herself staring into Damon Carrington's amused face. He was standing on her front porch, and he was holding a small, snub-nosed gun. The cold smile looked exactly like the one worn by the woman in the window, but with an indefinable difference.

"Hello, Elly. I was just about to knock. Something shake you up? You look nervous."

Instinctively, Elly flung herself backward into the safety of the house, intending to slam the door. But it was too late. Damon already had his foot over the threshold, and he lifted the gun in his hand with casual menace.

"Sorry, I'm afraid I can't let you run and hide. I need you tonight, Elly love. I've got plans for you. Keep in mind that I will use the gun if necessary. I'd prefer to keep you in reasonably good condition, but I can adapt to changing circumstances if there's no alternative. Translated, that means don't oblige me to put a bullet in your leg."

Elly's eyes jerked from the gun to Damon's face. Her voice felt dry and raspy. "That was you at the window?"

"In a way."

"What's that supposed to mean?" Elly demanded, using anger to hold back some of her fear. It wasn't Damon who answered.

"He means that the woman in the window was me." Blond hair cascading around her shoulders, Marina Carrington walked through Elly's front door.

There was no mistaking her. Elly knew her at once. She was a feminized version of Damon, right down to the amusement that flickered in her green eyes. She was wearing a black silk shirt and black slacks that presented a striking foil for the silvery blond hair. A pair of boots fashioned of obviously expensive leather completed the outfit. The clothes reminded Elly of a twentieth century version of a traditional witch's black cape and pointed shoes.

"All you lack is the hat," Elly muttered, hugging herself in an unconsciously defensive gesture.

"What hat?" Marina closed the door and examined Elly from head to toe. She didn't appear to be overly impressed.

"You know. Something with a broad brim and a point."

Marina tilted her head to one side, considering the comment and then she laughed. "Ah, a witch's hat. I see Jess has been discussing me with you."

"The subject came up after he saw you playing voyeur at my window."

"Shook him up a bit, did it? I'm not surprised. Always reassuring to know one hasn't been forgotten completely." Marina's eyes narrowed coolly. "But I don't suppose that's likely as long as he's amusing himself with boring women. His mind is bound to recall the good old days from time to time. Remember that the next time he decides to take you to bed. I gave him something a woman such as you will never be able to provide."

"A pain in the ass?"

Marina's fine teeth came together in a small snap. "You were right, Damon. She is a little bitch."

"Jess thinks you're dead," Elly said flatly, deciding the only thing she could do was keep talking.

"So does the insurance company," Damon said pleasantly. "They paid off very handsomely for the unfortunate loss of life at sea. We've been doing quite well on the income for the past three years. But now, sad to say, the money is running out."

Elly caught her breath, knowing what was coming. "Well, if you're thinking of supplementing your income by tapping my bank account, you're out of your mind. What I have saved wouldn't begin to keep you two in the style to which I'm sure you've become accustomed!"

Damon grinned. "It's not your money we're after, Elly. I think you know it."

Marina's grin mimicked her brother's and her eyes gleamed like those of a cat. "How much do you think Jess would pay to get you back safe and sound, Elly Trent? He seems to be quite fond of you. From what we hear he even plans to marry you."

Elly's fingers dug into her arms but she managed to keep her voice reasonably steady. "I don't see Jess paying ransom money."

"Then you don't know him very well," Marina informed her with vast assurance. "The man's got a streak of responsibility in him a yard wide. If he feels he got you into this mess, he'll do whatever he has to do to get you out."

Elly swallowed, aware that Marina was right in her assessment of Jess Winter. He was a man of integrity. He wouldn't send Elly to the wolves. But how would he react when he realized Marina was still alive?

"I can see why the two of you weren't compatible," Elly murmured, treating Marina to the same cool, analytical stare. "You obviously don't suffer from an excess of integrity."

"The man proved to be a little dull in some ways." Marina threw herself down into an arm chair. "But it was fun putting him through hoops for a while. Certainly did wonders for the family finances, didn't it, Damon?"

"Uh-huh." Damon motioned with the gun and Elly backed up a couple of steps.

"But unfortunately Jess had his limits. When I came up against them I knew the game was over." Marina eyed Elly again. "I wouldn't have expected him to settle for someone like you, however."

"Maybe you don't know him as well as you think you do."

Marina shook her head, a sardonic expression on her classically boned face. "You may be right. There were times when I wondered what he was really thinking, what made him tick. That generally doesn't happen. I can usually read a man's mind. Just as my brother always seems to know what a woman is thinking."

Elly swung her gaze to Damon, who was lounging near the telephone, the gun idly pointed in her direction. He was digging a slip of paper out of his pocket.

"Did you guess what I was thinking the other night when you sabotaged my car and then conveniently happened along that lonely road to 'rescue' me?" Elly dared.

Carrington's eyes slitted. "How did you know I was there? You'd already left by the time I arrived."

"I watched you from the bushes. I waited until you had given up and driven off before I walked home."

Damon's brows rose in mocking admiration. "Smarter than the average female. Well, at least I had the pleasure of throwing a scare into Winter. I'll bet he went crazy when he got my message."

"Did you do it just for spite?"

He shrugged. "Yeah. Seemed like fun. It would have been a convenient way of nabbing you. But no harm done. Everything's working out just fine, isn't it, Marina?"

"Beautifully," his sister agreed. "Are you ready to make the call?"

"Almost. This whole thing has to be properly timed. Tides, you know," he added helpfully as he glanced at Elly.

Elly's mouth went dry. Her tongue felt like sandpaper. "Tides? What about the tides?"

"You, my dear, are going to spend the night in a cozy little cabin a few miles from here," said Marina. "But tomorrow night you will spend it in a much more scenic location. You'll be able to watch the sun come up from a really choice vantage point." Marina languidly crossed one booted ankle over the other. "Go ahead and dial," she told Damon.

Elly stood frozen in front of the gun, watching in dull horror as Damon dialed the number on the slip of paper. It was Jess's number, she was certain of it. A moment later she was proved correct.

"We're all in luck," Damon said easily, without any preamble as Jess came on the line. "You're spending the evening at home. Elly will be delighted." There was a pause as Jess said something in response, and Damon's eyes filled with malicious amusement. "Of course she's here. I'm calling from her living room. Want to talk to her?" Without waiting for an answer he thrust the receiver toward Elly.

She took the instrument with shaking fingers. "Jess?"

"Christ, Elly, what the hell's going on?"

"The gruesome twosome has arrived on my doorstep," she managed to say, her tone as uneven as her grip on the phone.

"Twosome?"

The savage alertness in the single word told Elly all she needed to know about Jess's mood.

"Marina's not dead, Jess."

"That fits," he responded.

"With what?"

"Nothing, I'll explain later. Get rid of them, Elly. They're nothing but trouble. I want them out of your house now."

Elly glanced at the gun in Damon's fingers. "I couldn't agree with you more. Unfortunately, it's not going to be that simple. Damon has a gun, Jess. He's talking ransom."

The silence on the other end of the line seemed to reach out and chill Elly's entire living room. When Jess finally spoke he sounded unbelievably cold. "Are you all right?"

"Yes," she whispered.

"Put Carrington on the line."

Mutely, Elly handed the phone to Damon, who smiled as he spoke into the receiver. "As you can hear, she's in good health, Winter. And if everyone, especially you, follows orders, she'll stay that way. Marina and I aren't overly greedy. We just want what's coming to us. I'd say sweet little Elly here is worth about fifty thousand, wouldn't you?" He paused, listening. "No, I realize you can't lay your hands on that kind of money tonight. But you can get it first thing in the morning, can't you? The banks open at ten. We'll expect the cash to be packed neatly in a briefcase. You will drive here to Elly's house and wait for a phone call tomorrow evening. We will arrange the exchange at that time. Oh, and Winter. I probably don't have to spell this out, but I will for the sake of mutual understanding. Come alone. This is a small, isolated area. We're bound to notice if you bring the cops along for company. And if you do, Elly's going to disappear for good." Damon slammed down the receiver before there could be any further response.

"I think," said Marina, "that we'd better be on our way. Get a coat, Elly. You'll be spending the next twenty-four hours with us."

"Where?"

"At a deserted vacation cabin several miles from here. Damon and I have been staying there for the past few days, and so far no one's even noticed our presence. As long as we stay clear of town we're safe. It should be good for one more night. Now hurry up and get that coat unless you want to spend a very cold night."

"You don't have any heat at this cabin?" Elly asked as she obediently started to walk toward the hall closet. En route she had to pass the cluster of ivy plants on the bench against the wall. Beneath their cascading vines was the paring knife she had been using to trim dead leaves—the knife Jess had taken such pains to sharpen.

"Oh, the cabin is warm enough. But tomorrow night you're going to spend in a fairly uncomfortable situation, I'm afraid," Marina said smoothly. She watched Elly open the closet door and pull out a bulky down parka. "That should do the trick. Come on now, let's get going. Winter knows we called from your home. We don't want to give him time to mobilize the local cops, although I don't think he'll take the risk."

Elly stood clutching the parka, watching the other two uneasily. "But I don't understand," she began as she awkwardly started to struggle into the jacket. She made a production out of it, not bothering to fake her nervousness. It was quite real. "What will you do when you have the money? Jess won't let the matter rest. You know that. You know he'll find a way to track you down...."

She deliberately swung her arm wide as if having a problem fitting it into the parka sleeve.

The edge of the garment trailed along the row of ceramic ivy plant containers, knocking two of them off the edge of the table. With a haste that seemed impulsive and automatic, Elly turned to grab at the falling pots. She saw the paring knife as she swung around. For an instant her back was toward Damon and Marina. The sharp little knife disappeared up her sleeve even as the pots hit the floor with a jarring crash.

"You clumsy fool" Marina snapped, her eyes automatically following the small disaster. "Forget the damn plants and let's get going."

Turning slowly, her expression frightened and resentful, Elly shoved her hands into the pockets of her jacket and waited. Inside the right pocket she released the small knife.

"You'd better tie her wrists now, Marina." Damon removed a length of cord from his jacket and tossed it to his sister. "We wouldn't want her getting any clumsier."

Marina shook her head disgustedly as she stepped forward to tie Elly's hands behind her back. "Jess's standards have definitely slipped lately. I can't imagine what he sees in you. Stupid little country girl."

The knife seemed to be burning a hole in Elly's pocket, but Marina made no effort to search her. Why should she? The jacket had come straight out of the closet and couldn't be expected to have anything other than a stray tissue or some pennies tucked away in the pockets. "That's funny. Jess was just saying the other day that he can't remember what he ever saw in you," Elly remarked.

Marina gave the cord a vicious little jerk, and Elly immediately regretted the impulsive dig.

"Jess knows damn well what he saw in her," Damon said. "The same thing every other man sees in her. They all follow like lemmings to the sea."

"You didn't answer my question," Elly went on. She felt a little bolder now that it was becoming obvious Marina wasn't going to discover the knife. "What are you going to do when you have your hands on the money—assuming Jess brings the cash in the first place?"

"Oh, he'll bring it." Marina was serenely confident. "And he won't act until he has you safely back. That will give Damon and me plenty of time to leave the country." She glanced at her brother. "Ready?"

"All set. You drive and I'll keep an eye on Elly. Wouldn't want her to forget the position she's in."

Elly's gaze went from one incredibly attractive, determined face to the other, weighed the malice in the two sets of green eyes and knew she would be very lucky to get a chance to use the paring knife.

Damon grabbed one bound arm and led his victim toward the front door.

In Portland, Jess very carefully placed the receiver into its cradle. He didn't want to be careful with it. What he really wanted to do was hurl the damned instrument against the nearest off-white wall. The rage inside him was simmering so close to the surface it threatened to take over completely.

But the discipline of years did battle with the fury and won. There was nothing to be accomplished by blind rage at this point. The satisfaction of destruction would have to wait until later. So the phone was very carefully replaced. But Jess realized his fingers were almost shaking with the effort it took to control himself.

The Carringtons had dared to touch Elly.

Jess sat with his hands clenched between his knees, every muscle in his body screaming for action and revenge. The fools. Damon and Marina had played with fire so many times and gotten away with it so often that they no longer knew when to fear getting burned. Jess glanced at the neatly typed reports he had been studying when the phone had rung a few minutes earlier.

The papers carried the discrete, impressive letterhead of the very expensive, very efficient agency he had hired. It had cost a fortune, plus expenses, but the agency was convinced there was a high probability that Marina Carrington had not died in the yachting accident, and that she and her brother were alive and well and living very nicely on the coast of Mexico.

They should have had the sense to stay there, Jess decided as he got to his feet. They should have had the sense to keep clear of him and anything that belonged to him. But Damon and Marina had never been blessed with an overabundance of common sense. They saw no need to play by anyone else's rules. Until now, by and large, they had gotten away with their dangerous games.

Jess walked into the bedroom and found his briefcase. It appeared to be about the right size. He thought about what he knew of Damon and Marina. Both were inclined to be reckless, emotional, a little wild. They derived some kind of high from the turmoil and excitement they created around them. They fed on the trouble they caused the way a shark feeds on the smaller fish around it. But the fact that they got their kicks from creating trouble was also their chief weakness, unless you counted the strange bond between the twins. They were two halves of a whole, functioning at times almost like a single entity. That, too, could be a weakness. Jess contemplated the thought for a while.

In a way he understood the link better now than he ever had in the past. During the time he had known Elly, a silent bond had been formed, the strength of which he had only recently begun to comprehend. With the instincts of natural predators, the Carringtons had found his main weakness. Jess would do whatever he had to in order to see Elly safe. To Damon and Marina, Elly probably appeared to be a weak point through which they could reach Jess. What they didn't realize was that she had also become a source of strength to him.

There was nothing to do now but wait. For a moment he stood quietly, picturing Elly bound and helpless in the Carringtons' hands.

Once again the savage rage simmered to the surface, almost swamping him, and once again Jess controlled it. He would get Elly free first. Then he would deal with Damon and Marina Carrington. This time he would see to it that they were finally consumed by the fire they had started.

Fire was reputed to be the one sure way of dealing with witches.

Elly was uncomfortable, stiff and disgusted. Fear had given way to other emotions as time passed. Nothing was working out the way it did in the movies. She had expected to be tossed into a closet or a bedroom and left by herself. At that point she could have begun industrious work with the paring knife. Instead she had been kept seated on a worn-out couch in the main room of the small beach cabin in full sight of the Carringtons. Even asking to use the bathroom facilities had not brought her any solitude. Marina had accompanied her, bringing the gun along.

The little knife continued to burn a hole in her jacket. The only measure of satisfaction she had was that she hadn't been told to remove the garment.

When it became apparent that Damon and Marina had decided to take turns staying awake during the night, Elly finally decided to try getting some sleep. After several restless attempts she finally succeeded.

She awoke a long time later, vaguely aware of the low murmur of the twins' voices as they sat talking near the fire. For a moment Elly didn't try to concentrate on what they were saying. For one thing, her arms ached and she had developed a headache from her awkward sleeping position. It seemed more trouble than it was worth to make the effort to shift her position. She lay still, eyes closed and wondered what Jess was doing.

She knew, just as the Carringtons appeared to know, that he would come for her. He would pay whatever price was necessary. That fact depressed Elly more than anything else that had happened. Once again he would assume his responsibilities. Once again he would endeavor to bail Elly out of trouble. She longed to make him aware of a wild, passionate love he had for her and all she succeeded in doing was finding odd little ways of drawing out his sense of responsibility and integrity—if you could call getting yourself kidnapped an odd little way of doing things. When this was all over would he finally decide she was too much trouble?

There I go again, Elly thought morosely. *I'm acting nervous and afraid of having pushed him too far.* What she had to remember was that this kidnapping, at least, was hardly her fault. Unless, she decided on a wave of uneasy guilt, it might have been prevented by telling Jess earlier that Damon Carrington was still hanging around. No use letting her thoughts drift too far in that direction. What was done was done. The low voices near the fire filtered slowly into her mind.

"We'll arrange the pickup to be here at the cabin," Damon was saying quietly. "We'll be able to see if any cars other than Winter's Jaguar come near. If they do we'll know he's been followed."

"He won't go to the cops," Marina said with amused certainty. "He'll handle this by himself."

"Just in case, one of us will stay out of sight when he arrives with the money. I'll pick up the briefcase and we'll make him think you're guarding little miss wholesome over there. He won't move on one of us as long as he thinks the other has Elly."

Marina laughed softly. "She won't be needing any guard out on that rock. I'll wait in the car for you. In the time it takes Jess to figure out where sweet little Elly is and call in the cops, we'll be on a plane out of Portland. We can be safely out of the country before anyone figures out which direction we've gone."

The word *rock* worried Elly more than anything else that had happened so far. She had been subconsciously working on the assumption that the Carringtons hadn't progressed to the point of contemplating murder. Maybe she was wrong. That realization sent the first of several cold chills down her spine.

But the real chills began much later that day when she finally realized what was in store for her. The short twilight was falling across the ocean when the Carringtons finally jostled her into the Porsche.

"I'm going to hate leaving this baby behind," Damon said, patting the leather-bound steering wheel.

"You can get another."

"The fifty thousand isn't going to go far if I start out using most of it to buy another car." Damon frowned as he turned the vehicle down a back road that led close to the beach.

"We'll get it on credit. We can make the fifty thousand look like five hundred thousand to a potential creditor. Look how long we made that insurance money last," Marina reminded him. She was the one holding the gun now. She kept it loosely aligned with Elly's midsection. When the fifty thousand is gone we'll think of something else."

"We always do," Damon agreed with a strange smile.

"It keeps life interesting." Marina smiled at Elly. "You should be grateful to us. This is probably the most excitement you've ever had. Enjoy it."

"I can live without your brand of excitement."

Marina laughed. "That's what Jess eventually decided, too. Wonder what he's thinking now that he's having to cope with it again."

Elly looked away, not bothering to answer. Her mind was filled now with the path Damon was taking to the sea. It would be totally dark soon, but she knew where they were. They were nearing the cove that was less than a mile from her home—the cove that contained the castle rock. Elly remembered what had been said earlier about leaving her on the rock. Then she frantically tried to recall the tide schedule. A new kind of fear began building in her.

"This should be it," Damon announced, parking the Porsche at the edge of the bluff. "Let's get moving. I don't want to stay out here in the open any longer than necessary."

"It's getting dark," Marina pointed out. "No one can see us."

"Still, I don't like it." He reached for Elly, pulling her out of the car so abruptly that she stumbled and fell to her knees. "Get up, bitch." He glanced at his twin. "Got the rest of that rope?"

"I've got it."

"Give it to me. I'll take care of this." He yanked Elly across the wet sand, pushing her toward the castle rock. "I hear you don't like salt water, Elly, love. In fact, I gather you have a real fear of swimming in the sea. In another couple of hours that's the only way you'll be able to get off that rock. That's assuming you found some way to untie yourself first, which isn't very likely, is it? Besides, I got a good look at this place the other day when I brought Sarah and her brat down here. When the tide is in, even a good swimmer would have trouble with those waves. Even after we tell him where you are, Winter probably won't be able to get you off until morning."

Elly flinched as she stared straight ahead. The sea was already beginning to foam around the base of the rock. It licked eagerly at her feet as Damon forced her toward the encrusted fortress. In another hour the waves would be crashing roughly and the water would be waist deep in the imaginary moat that protected the castle. In two hours it would be over her head and pounding the cove violently. Only the tip of the rock would remain above the water. If it stormed, even that position would be untenable.

"This is hardly necessary, Damon," she tried to argue calmly. "Why not leave me tied up on shore? I'm not going anywhere with both hands and feet tied."

"Just an added precaution. I don't want any surprises. Marina and I have this planned down to the minute, and I don't want anything happening to alter our plans. And," he added with an evil grin, "it appeals to my sense of humor."

"Leaving me stranded here? You've got a very distorted sense of humor."

"I know. But it helps keep life amusing. Move, Elly." He forced her into the ankle-deep water, chuckling when she instinctively recoiled. He motioned for her to start climbing to the top of the rocky castle.

Elly tried not to think about the crunching sound her feet made as she slithered and slipped on the shells of the small creatures clinging to the sides of their private fortress. When she had to grip the rocky surface in order to keep her balance, her hand came in contact with something that moved hurriedly out of the way, and she almost screamed.

"Hurry up, Elly. I haven't got all night."

She wanted to plead with her captor and knew it would be useless. He would only derive more pleasure out of what he was doing to her. Grimly, Elly tried to push her imagination to the furthest corners of her mind while she finished the awkward scramble. In a few more minutes she wouldn't be able to see much at all, and then what would she do when the small things skittered and darted in and around the rocky pile they called home?

Ten minutes later Elly sat alone, imprisoned queen of the castle, and watched the lights of the Porsche disappear. Below her the sea began to surge more and more impatiently around the base of the fortress.

Elly decided she could certainly understand why the Carringtons' brand of excitement had begun to pall on Jess.

Nine

It was when she began fumbling for the paring knife that Elly realized there were other aspects of her situation that didn't fit the movie stereotype. It was damned hard to work her bound hands around to the pocket on the side of her jacket—especially when the sound of the sea and the silence of her fellow inmates kept distracting her.

She was sitting on a reasonably level surface of the rock, a position that would have been visible if someone had happened by on the bluff above the beach. And if it had been daylight.

Her fingers seemed to have grown rather numb, although Marina hadn't tied her wrists tight enough to cut off circulation. Perhaps it was the cold evening air that was causing the lack of feeling.

Something moved around her toes, probably a small crab. Elly jerked her bound feet away and felt her ankle scrape across a rough-edged shell. It was impossible in the dim light to tell if she had cut herself, but Elly was very much afraid she had. The thought panicked her for an instant. Would blood draw more of the rock's denizens?

She mustn't think about that. She had to focus every ounce of concentration on getting free. Soon the rendezvous between Damon and Jess would take place, and if there was to be any hope of resolving this mess she had to get off the rock. Damned if she would let Jess shell out fifty thousand dollars for her. And damned if she would let the Carringtons get away with using her to get at their old enemy.

The paring knife came into her fingers at last. It seemed slippery as she drew it carefully from her pocket, and her initial fear was that she would drop it and never find it again in the darkness.

Cautiously, she grasped the knife's handle and tried to angle the blade toward the cords that bound her wrists. She made contact easily enough, but there was no magical parting of the strands. Instead she seemed to be sawing away uselessly. The knife had been dulled by her insistence on using it on her plants. Jess had been right. You never knew when you were going to need a sharp knife.

Chagrined, Elly closed her eyes in frustration and wondered how she would make excuses the next time she saw Jess. Contemplation of that gave her the energy to continue sawing on the cords. Surely there was some cutting edge left on the blade. Jess had spent time and care sharpening it. With a growing sense of desperation, she continued working away at the cords and finally something began to give.

She was making some progress, Elly realized. The knowledge gave her the courage to continue.

The process took far longer than she would have expected. By the time Elly's wrists were freed and she started in on the ankle ties, she was chilled and tired. Her muscles ached from the constant pressure of trying to cut through the bonds, and her jeans were damp from the restless spray of the incoming waves. The knowledge that the spray was already leaping as high as her perch told Elly just how deep the water around her was becoming. Frantically, she renewed her efforts and cried out in shock and rage a moment later when the frail knife finally snapped.

"Damn it to hell!" Tossing aside the useless handle, Elly leaned down to wrench at the remaining cords. Perhaps they had already been nearly severed, or perhaps her fear and anger made her stronger than she knew. In any event, she was finally free a few moments later.

She scrambled to a kneeling position, wincing as her palms found the wet, rough surface of the rock. Her legs were chilled and so were her hands. Thank God for the goosedown parka.

There was only one way down from the top of the castle and that was the same way she had climbed it. It was either that or cower up here until Jess finally found her.

The thought of Jess searching for her sent Elly over the side. Once again she closed her ears to the awful crunching sounds. When she accidentally came into contact with a scurrying crab she inhaled sharply, but she didn't lose her grip. The stupid crab could just get out of the way, she told herself resolutely. Five more minutes and she would be off his house.

The hardest part came when her feet slipped into the foaming surface of the water. She was startled at the strength of the surging tide.

"Well, at least it's headed in the right direction," she told herself aloud in hopes of arousing another drop or two of courage. "I won't be carried out to sea. I'll be washed ashore."

Being battered about on the rocks didn't sound like a heck of a good alternative, however. Elly clung to the wall of the castle and tried to remember exactly what the terrain around her looked like when it wasn't inundated with water. Slowly the picture formed in her mind. While she thought about it, she remembered to unzip her down jacket. She should try to keep it as dry as possible. She was going to need it when she got to shore. She would be chilled to the bone from the cold sea. She tied it awkwardly around her throat.

To her right there was a shoulder of rock that contained several pitted areas. They could prove treacherous footing. She inched to the left and lowered herself a little farther. She was seeking the sandy bottom at the base of the fortress. How had the water become so deep so quickly? She was losing track of time.

She found the bottom with jolting force when a playful wave ripped her free of the rock and tossed her toward shore. Elly floundered, trying to right herself and staggered violently when her foot touched bottom. The water was up to her waist. She was soaked. Her clothing and her shoes seemed to be deadweights trying to drag her under.

Once again she remembered the possibility of her ankle having been cut earlier. Primitive fears of sharks and other creatures being drawn by blood sent Elly splashing desperately for shore. The swirling water caught at her, playing with her, terrifying her, but it didn't succeed in tripping her. For a split second she almost considered climbing back up the rock.

Closing her eyes against the salty sting of the sea, she again pictured the terrain in her mind. When she risked lifting her lashes again, she knew where she was and what she had to do in order to get to shore.

Jess would be frantic worrying about her, and he would be in danger from the twins. Elly had no alternative but to get to shore—just as she'd had no alternative that day so long ago when she'd gone into the sea to rescue Dave. When there was no alternative, you did what had to be done.

The struggle to the beach seemed to last forever, and it drained so much energy that by the time she reached the damp sand Elly could hardly stand. She wavered for a moment trying to savor her victory, but she was beyond any thoughts of triumph. There was a vast sense of relief but that was it.

She was so cold. She had never been so cold. The sudden fear of hypothermia made her untie the damp jacket. Hastily, she shrugged into it. It provided the warmth the core of her body needed. Knowing there was no longer any time to waste, Elly turned in the direction of her home. She would take time later to congratulate herself on the battle with the sea.

The only goal in her life right now was to get to the beach cottage before Damon and Marina got away with using wholesome little Elly Trent against Jess. As she jogged heavily down the beach, Elly realized she didn't feel very sweet or wholesome at all tonight. She felt like committing murder.

The house was deserted when she reached it. If Jess had come there to wait for the phone call, he had already received it and left. The front door was unlocked, Elly discovered. He must have left in a hurry. Not like Jess to overlook details.

She walked into the front room and stood there dripping while she examined the scene. Jess had been there, all right. A half-empty glass stood on the table in front of the sofa. It didn't appear to contain Scotch, however. It looked more like mineral water.

Jess wouldn't have risked dulling his reactions with alcohol, Elly decided. Not when he was on his way to meet Damon Carrington. Hastily, she stripped off her jeans and wet clothing, dashing up the stairs as she did so. Grabbing for dry clothes in her closet, she put them on with the same fumbling haste. Then she was racing back down the stairs. The car keys were sitting on the table in the hall where she always left them. She had them in her hand and was out the door in seconds.

Halfway to her destination Elly belatedly began to wonder if she shouldn't have called the local authorities. Well, it was too late now to have second thoughts. She pushed the accelerator closer to the floor. She would have to leave the car some distance from the beach cottage or the Carringtons would be warned of her approach. She knew exactly where to put the vehicle. She'd place it squarely across the road that Damon would take when he and Marina started for Portland.

Parking the car where she had intended, Elly abandoned it and started toward the cabin. With any luck the distant rumble of the sea would hide any noise she might make as she approached. It wasn't until she rounded a corner and saw the tail of the Porsche in her path that she remembered Marina was supposed to be waiting in the car. The thought brought Elly to an abrupt halt.

Changing her direction, she slipped into the trees alongside the road and stayed out of the sight of anyone sitting in the Porsche. As she went past, she thought she saw Marina's blond head in the driver's seat. Elly went on toward the cabin.

The white Jaguar was sitting in the driveway. Elly halted again, uncertain of what to do next. There were lights on inside the old house. Slowly, she approached from one side. When she reached a window she realized she was looking into the main room.

Jess was standing there, the briefcase at his feet. He looked deceptively casual, as if he were only talking business. It was Damon who looked nervous. He was holding the gun very tightly, not with the studied ease he'd used when aiming it at Elly. His evident tension told Elly all she needed to know.

Damon might be reckless and dangerous, but he was also smart enough to be scared. He'd gotten himself in fairly deep this time, and he seemed to be realizing it. So did Jess. Elly couldn't hear his muffled voice through the window, but she could hear Damon's. The younger man's words were too loud and too sharp—further evidence of his unstable emotional state.

"Don't you dare threaten me, Winter. Not if you want to see your precious little country girl again. Believe me, it will be easy enough for Marina to leave her where she is. You'll never find her in time to save her unless I tell you where we've put her. So just shut your damn mouth and open that briefcase. I want to see the money."

Jess said something quietly in response. Elly couldn't make it out, but she saw him go down slowly on one knee to open the briefcase.

Unable to think of anything else to do, Elly yelled through the window, "Hey, Carrington! If you think we're going to let you have that money, you're..." She didn't get any further.

Elly wasn't at all surprised when Damon whirled to face the window with a shocked expression. She had meant to get his attention. But she was more than a little startled to see him raise the gun with deadly purposefulness. He'd clearly panicked at the sight of her. Realizing belatedly that he was going to pull the trigger, Elly threw herself down onto the cold ground.

The gun roared and the window shattered as the bullet tore through it. Elly ducked her head instinctively, staying down. But there was no second shot. She heard Damon's violent yell from inside the cottage and then the sound of crashing furniture.

"Elly!"

She glanced up from her crouching position to see Jess leaning out the window, an expression of savage concern on his face.

"I'm all right, Jess,"

He didn't wait. Instead he turned back into the room before she could move.

Alarmed at the thought of what might be happening, Elly leaped to her feet and stared at the scene in front of her. Clearly Jess had jumped Carrington in the same moment the other man had pulled the trigger. The impact of his lunge had sent Damon crashing up against the wall, stunning him. Now the two men were sprawling across the floor in a short, violent battle that was ending almost as soon as it began. Damon didn't stand a chance.

The gun had been sent flying in the first assault and Jess's sheer fury had taken care of the rest. With a ferocity that left Elly wide-eyed and voiceless, he pinned his younger opponent to the floor and started to hammer at Damon's beautifully chiseled face.

Damon's cries of pain became mere grunts and then faded altogether. Elly realized he was almost unconscious from the punishment. She darted around the corner of the house and dashed through the front door.

"Jess! Jess, that's enough, you'll kill him!"

Her voice seemed to break the raging anger that was dominating Jess. He went still above his victim and his burning eyes swung to Elly.

"You're all right." It was a statement, not a question.

Elly nodded and finally found her voice again. "I'm okay, Jess."

"I should kill him."

"He's not worth it. Let the law have him. Besides, we've got Marina to worry about." Desperately she tried to distract him with mention of the other twin. The thought of Jess killing a man because of her was more than Elly wanted to contend with just then. There would be endless inquiries and explanations. Perhaps worse. She'd already caused her lover enough trouble. Her only goal now was to end this mess before it got any more difficult.

It was something of a joke when you thought about it, she decided. She was always trying to keep Jess from becoming embroiled in trouble on her behalf, and all she accomplished was another disaster.

"Marina! Christ, I almost forgot about her." Jess staggered to his feet, wiping a trace of blood off his mouth. "Where is she?"

"In the Porsche outside."

"He said she was guarding you."

"He lied. They stuck me on that rock in the middle of the cove."

Jess's eyes narrowed. "The tide..."

"I know. I'll tell you about it later. Right now we've got to stop Marina." Even as Elly spoke the roar of the Porsche's engine split the night.

"She's leaving! Damn that witch. I swear to God, this time I'm going to put these two away for ten years."

"Damon probably told her to get out if she heard gunfire and he didn't immediately appear. But she's not going far. I parked my car across the road."

Jess swung around, one brow lifting. "You're just full of surprises tonight, aren't you? Come on, help me with handsome over there."

"What are you going to do?"

"Use him to stop Marina."

Jess ignored the small handgun on the floor and knelt down to open his briefcase. From inside he withdrew a wicked-looking weapon of his own. It gleamed a dull blue-black in the cabin light. Elly stared at it.

"What on earth? I thought you had money in there!"

"I do. I also had this. Come on, let's get Carrington on his feet."

He reached down to haul Damon upright. Carrington was so groggy he didn't seem to realize who was bracing him or what was happening. When he was forced to move toward the door of the cabin, he groaned but he didn't argue. Elly drew his arm around her shoulder to steady him while Jess kept him on his feet.

In the darkness outside, the Porsche headlights cut a swath through the night as the car swung violently around on the narrow road. Marina had just realized the exit was blocked. She was starting back toward the cabin. As she gunned the sportscar's engine, Jess pushed Damon out into the middle of her path. The injured man staggered and fell to the ground.

Simultaneously the Porsche's tires screamed as the brakes were applied with savage force. Then the car door opened.

"Damon!" Marina ran toward her brother. "Damon!"

"Stay right where you are, Marina, or I'll put a bullet in him. Maybe one in you, too, for that matter. I'm really getting sick of Carringtons." Jess stepped out of the trees. The lights of the car fell harshly on the gun in his hand. "This time I think I'm going to do more than just hope you'll stay out of my life. This time I'm going to do something permanent to make certain you stay out of it."

"You hurt him! You hurt Damon!"

"He hurt Elly," Jess responded in a voice as cold as his surname. "He's lucky I didn't kill him and you both. Believe me, the temptation to finish this right here and now is overwhelming. Don't tempt me, Marina."

Kneeling beside her brother in the glare of the headlights, Marina looked up at Jess. Perhaps it was the harsh light or perhaps it was the equally harsh expression on her face; for whatever reason she didn't seem very beautiful just then. Elly felt almost sorry for her. Marina Carrington appeared to be finally comprehending the fact that this time she might have gone too far.

"You can't prove anything, Jess," Marina said in a last-ditch effort. "It'll be your word against ours."

"If I have trouble making the kidnapping charges stick, we'll see how well the insurance company does with its fraud charges. On your feet, Marina. We've got a lot to do."

Something moved on Marina's face as she stared at him. Her voice softened, took on a gently pleading note. "Jess . . . Jess, please. Listen to me. For the sake of what we once . . ."

"Forget it, Marina. That act hasn't worked in a long time. You wore it out with too many performances. That's your whole problem, you know, as well as your brother's. You were born thinking you could get away with anything forever. But you pushed your luck a little too far this time. You had the stupidity to threaten something I want very badly. Stupidity is the one crime for which you always have to pay in this world."

"Bastard," Marina hissed, the softness leaving instantly as she took in the unwavering set of his face.

Jess smiled faintly. "Now you've got it, Marina."

It was much later that evening when a subdued, watchful Elly sat sipping the brandy Jess had just poured. She had spoken very little to him during the past two hours. In truth there hadn't been much opportunity. The local law authorities hadn't experienced any difficulty in believing Jess's side of the tale. After all, Deputy Charlie Atkins knew Jess and Elly. In a small town the burden of proof tended to be on the outsiders, not on the locals who filed the complaints against them.

Besides, as Charlie took pains to explain to his superior, there were those Porsche tracks on the bluff above the cove, all that money in a briefcase and Elly Trent's wet clothes. Everybody knew Elly Trent wouldn't go swimming voluntarily. In point of fact nobody in his right mind went swimming in a cold sea at night. In addition, everyone in town knew Jess and Elly. Good people. They wouldn't make up a thing like this. Charlie's boss concurred.

Elly turned over in her mind the scene in the sheriff's office as she watched Jess pour his own glass of brandy. He hadn't settled down yet. There was a tension in him that wasn't dissolving, even though the Carringtons were safely in custody. When he'd finished pouring the brandy, he picked up the glass and began pacing the room in front of her. Elly curled her legs beneath her as she sat on the sofa. Her wariness increased.

"How did you know about the insurance fraud?" she finally asked. She had been trying for several minutes to think of something to break the taut silent.

Jess took a sip of his brandy. "I had a firm working on it. The report was waiting for me when I got back to the apartment yesterday."

"An investigation firm?"

"Yeah."

Elly frowned. "But how did you know? I mean, what made you hire a detective agency?"

"After Damon showed up here I decided to do a little checking. I knew he was up to something, and it made me wonder how he'd been surviving on his own for the past three years. He and Marina had always functioned as a team—a pair of wolves who hunted together. I made a few inquiries and learned he'd been out of the country until recently. That made me even more suspicious. Why stay away from the States that long? And if he really felt

I'd been somehow responsible for Marina's death, why didn't he come looking for revenge before now? I kept the inquiries going." Jess shrugged, pausing by the fireplace. "One thing led to another. The investigators turned up fairly convincing evidence that Marina was still alive."

"I see."

"I got Carrington's call just as I'd finished reading the report."

It seemed to Elly there was a trace of accusation in his words. Jess swung around to face her, his thumb hooked into the waistband of the jeans he was wearing. Out of force of habit she almost began to apologize. She stopped herself just as the words trembled on her lips. "Thank you for coming to my rescue," she said instead, her voice very formal.

Jess stared at her thoughtfully. "You were doing a pretty good job of rescuing yourself. I'm proud of you, Elly. When I think of how you must have felt trapped on that damn rock with the tide coming in I could strangle both Carringtons. Was it very bad?"

"It was..." she hesitated, seeking the appropriate word, "manageable. The worse part actually turned out to be the cold. That's why I had to change clothes before driving to the beach house."

Jess shook his head, looking appalled. "How did you get free? I thought they had you tied hand and foot."

Elly cleared her throat. "Yes. Well, Jess, thereby hangs a very interesting tale. Remember that little paring knife you said I shouldn't use for trimming the plants and digging around in the dirt?"

He eyed her with sudden alertness. "I remember."

"It, uh, happened to be sitting conveniently over there under the ivy. When Marina ordered me to put on my coat I was a little clumsy and managed to knock off those pots you see on the floor. When I pretended to try to catch them I palmed the knife." She smiled widely. "Brilliant, huh?"

Jess lifted his eyes heavenward in silent supplication. "I won't ask how the knife got to be under the ivy. I'll just be grateful that it was."

"Look on the bright side, Jess. If you hadn't sharpened it recently it probably wouldn't have cut through the cords at all."

"I'll take comfort in that." He began to pace. "I won't take any comfort in the memory of the way you jumped up on the other side of that window at the beach house, though. Damn it to hell, Elly, Carrington could have killed you. He was a stick of dynamite waiting to explode, and when you distracted him he lost control. Not to mention what you did to my frame of mind."

Elly heard the beginning of the censuring tone again and stirred restlessly on the couch. "Now, Jess..."

"By the way," he went on ruthlessly, really warming to his theme now, "the deputy said he heard that Carrington put in an appearance at that potluck you went to last week. You never mentioned seeing him."

Elly coughed faintly. "I didn't see any point in saying anything. It would only have upset you and besides, I—"

"Upset me! Elly, if I'd known he was still in the neighborhood I could have taken some action. I could have protected you better. As it was, I was sitting blithely in Portland thinking there was no immediate concern. You should have told me he was still in town."

"I was trying to avoid an embarrassing and possibly dangerous confrontation."

"What did you get instead? An extremely dangerous confrontation." He swung around sharply, starting toward the far side of the room. His dark brows formed a solid line above his gray eyes. "I know the present situation is resolved, but this whole mess only goes to show that it's time I stepped up the schedule. I don't want to spend any more evenings than absolutely necessary sitting alone in Portland wondering what you're doing. My nerves won't tolerate it. We've wasted enough time. There's no reason we can't be married next week. I can wind up my last consulting job by Friday and move in here with you on Saturday. Once I'm finally living here I won't have to worry about what's going on all week."

Elly's cautious nature began to disintegrate. "Now hold on just a minute, Jess."

He ignored her, lost in his plans. "I can contact a moving company tomorrow. We can also apply for the license this week. I'll arrange for the ceremony on Monday. You might want to have a few friends in for a reception or something. That's fine with me. In the meantime, I'll get my consulting reports out of the way."

"Damn it, Jess, just slow down for one blessed minute!" Elly leaped to her feet, her eyes blazing as her temper and her wariness collided in a small internal explosion. "This is my life we're discussing, not just yours, and I've got a couple of things to say about it."

Wanting to quell her tirade, he slanted her a glance. "Calm down, Elly, I'm just making a few plans."

"You're shuffling me around on that damned schedule of yours, and I'm not sure I want to be shuffled. Sit down, Jess Winter, I've got something to say." She advanced on him, her fists planted on her hips. "Go on, sit down!"

"Elly, you've been through a lot tonight. You're probably feeling tired and you're still under a strain."

"I'm not in a mood to be soothed or consoled or patted on the head and sent to bed. Sit down, Jess." She was too wound up to be surprised when he did exactly as she ordered. Warily, he sank down onto the couch and took another sip of brandy. She stood facing him determinedly. "Now, let's get specific about these plans of yours. In case you hadn't noticed, my whole future is at stake here. And I have a few comments I'd like to make."

"I'm listening."

"I accused you of being afraid to let yourself love me. I decided you were running scared."

"Elly..."

She held up a hand. "But I had it all backward, Jess Winter. I'm the one who's running scared. I've been nervous and wary and...and cautious around you since day one. I was afraid of pushing you on the physical side of things, so I spent weeks agonizing over the reason you didn't ask me to go to bed with you. You always seemed to be on some sort of schedule, and I was afraid of disrupting it. After I finally worked up my nerve to try the big seduction scene and had it so rudely interrupted by Marina, I began fretting over the fact that I might say or do something to remind you of her. Then I saw you face to face with Damon, and I worried that if I didn't keep you two apart there would be violence."

"Elly, let me—"

"I'm not finished yet. When my family business problems became pressing, I panicked about you involving yourself for fear it would bring up more memories of your experiences with the Carringtons. I've been getting increasingly nervous about the fact that you can't seem to admit you love me. That, Jess, is the last straw."

Jess suddenly went still. "What are you saying, Elly?"

"That I'm through running scared—through being wary, through walking on eggs around you when it comes to sticky issues. I'm not going to let you make me nervous or afraid any longer. I'm giving you an ultimatum. I'm not going to fit conveniently into your schedule anymore, Jess. We're not getting married until you find the guts to admit you love me. And you're going to have to make me believe it."

Ten

Y̆ou do? You know?'' The room had been fraught with silence when Elly finally spoke.

"I know."

Elly stared at him. Jess's mouth crooked slightly as he glanced down into his brandy and then back up to meet her eyes. He didn't elaborate. She continued to stare at him, finally remembering to close her mouth.

"You do?" she managed weakly. She felt as if the fire that had been driving her had suddenly flamed out. "How long have you... I mean, when did you decide you loved me?"

"I think I've known since the beginning," Jess said with a strange gentleness. "You were so very right in every way. Before I realized what I was doing I was fitting you into all my plans. I couldn't schedule my future without you. But I didn't want to spell it all out to myself. You were right in that regard, too. I was running scared."

"Oh, Jess, I didn't really mean that."

"Sure you did, it's the truth. I've been coming to terms with it for quite a while, ever since you tried to stage your sweet seduction act. But I wasn't ready to talk about it in San Francisco. I was still trying to come to terms with it myself. I've spent too many years learning to be in control, Elly. I wanted to be in control of myself and of everything around me. I think I've always been inclined to be that way, but after that fiasco of a marriage with Marina I really decided to stay in command of myself and others. Never again was I going to let myself get strung out the way I did with her. I made a total fool of myself. That's a hard thing for a man to live down, Elly."

Elly was consumed with remorse for having pushed him into the confession. She rushed forward, throwing herself onto her knees in front of him. Catching one of his big hands between hers, she looked up at him earnestly. "I know, Jess. I thought that was the problem. I should never have provoked you into admitting it. You have every right to deal with this in your own way and in your own time. Forget I said anything, okay?"

He looked amused. "It's too late. You've already said it. And so have I."

"Well, we'll just pretend that you haven't."

"The hell we will." His eyes were warming with a sensual laughter. He set down the brandy glass and moved his free hand to her braided hair. "One of the things you're going to have to learn, Elly, is that if you insist on pushing a man to the wall, you have to take the consequences."

"What consequences?"

"You said I was not only going to have to admit I loved you, but make you believe I meant it."

"I believe you. I have to believe you, Jess. I love you so múch I just knew you loved me, too. Or that you'd love me if you just gave yourself a chance. That's what I was really afraid of, you know," she added confidingly. "I was terrified you'd take what I offered and resist . . . well, you know what I mean."

"You'd thought I'd take everything you had to give and resist surrendering in return."

Hurriedly Elly denied that. "It wasn't that you didn't give me a lot in return. You did, Jess. For one thing I trust you, and that means more than I can ever say. You're an honorable man and you're generous. You even tolerated my obnoxious relatives. And you've definitely managed to reassure me that you want me. You have given me a lot."

"But it wasn't quite enough to make you agree to marry me." Slowly, Jess began to work loose one of the pins that held her braids in place.

"I guess I'm a greedy woman," Elly admitted humbly.

"Mmm." He removed the next pin. "I'm glad."

"You are?"

"Definitely. Elly, my love, if you and events in general hadn't pushed me a little during the past couple of weeks, I might have taken months getting around to acknowledging my own feelings. What a waste that would have been."

She smiled gently. "Why?"

"Because I've decided I like admitting that I love you. It's a great relief, you see. I no longer have to worry about maintaining my control when it comes to you. I began realizing that after the first time I took you to bed. Everything felt good afterward. It felt right. Now I know I can just relax and surrender to the inevitable. I don't have to worry about the end results. You taught me not to fear them, sweetheart. I owe you for that. And I intend to spend the rest of my life thanking you.''

"You do?''

"Beginning right now,'' he assured her. Under his deft touch more pins came free from her hair, and a moment later the braids tumbled down around her shoulders. "I love to take your hair down, Elly. There's something so full of promise about the whole thing.'' He threaded his fingers through the chestnut strands, loosening them until they cascaded over his hands. "I want you, Elly.''

"I'm glad,'' she said simply, her eyes brimming with her love. "Because I love you so much, Jess.''

His palm cupped her face as he looked down at her with an intensity that took away her breath. "In the beginning I told myself you had nothing to worry about because I would take good care of your love. I promised myself I would treasure it, protect it, keep it safe. Now I know that I want to give as much as I get.''

She caught his hand and turned her lips into the warm palm. "I'll treasure your love, Jess. I'll protect it and keep it safe.''

"I know. I trust you, Elly. I've never really trusted a woman before in my life. But I trust you.''

She looked up at him, aware of the depth of truth in his words. She decided to take the risk of clearing up one last point. "Once you called me a witch. It was that first night we made love. Remember? We argued afterward and you called me a witch.''

"Did I?" Jess didn't seem particularly interested. He was lifting her to her feet and standing up beside her. Strong hands settled on her shoulders. "That worried you?"

"Because it's what you always called Marina."

"There are two kinds of witchcraft, my sweet Elly. Haven't you read enough fairy tales to know that? Believe me, I've learned about both kinds the hard way. From Marina I learned about the dark, destructive sort. But you taught me about the other kind—the kind associated with sunlight and life and love. There's no one who's more certain of the truth than a man who's seen both the false and the real. Trust me to know the difference, honey."

She wrapped her arms around his waist, resting her head on his shoulder. "I trust you, Jess."

He bent and scooped her up in his arms. "While we're on the subject of trust," he began as he strode toward the stairs with her in his arms, "this is probably a good time to mention that I don't particularly want to be protected from certain facts in the future. I want you to trust me completely, Elly."

Elly lifted her head. "Do I hear a lecture coming on? Something pithy about the way I neglected to mention Damon's lingering presence in the community?"

"You're very perceptive, sweetheart." He reached the top of the stairs and turned toward Elly's bedroom.

"I hope you're not going to get into the habit of lecturing me every time you carry me off to bed. It could spoil the mood, you know. Might give me a headache." She let her fingers slide persuasively up to the nape of neck.

"I have an excellent home remedy for headaches." He stood her on her feet and removed the burnt-orange sweater she was wearing. It came free in one easy sweep of his hands and his eyes shadowed with desire as he touched the tips of her breasts. "Guaranteed not to fail."

She felt herself growing warm with the beginnings of sensual tension at the husky tone of his voice. "Unfortunately, I don't have a headache so we won't be able to experiment with your remedy."

"Then we'll go straight to bed. I'll get back to the lecture later." He undressed her with an urgency that told its own story, his fingers trembling slightly as he stroked her.

Elly fumbled with his shirt until it joined the growing pile of clothing on the floor, and then she unfastened his jeans. As the last garment fell away, he pushed himself into her hands, letting her know the full weight and readiness of his need.

"Elly, my sweet, exciting Elly." He picked her up again and settled her on the bed. "Do you know what I regret most about the last couple of months?"

"What's that?" She reached for him as he came down beside her.

"I regret my own stupidity in waiting so long to take you to bed. When I think of all the nights together we missed..." His words broke off as he leaned down to kiss the swell of her breast. Then his hand tightened on her hip. "I could kick myself."

"That's what you get for being so schedule-conscious."

"Don't sound so smug. There's a lot to be said for schedules. I'm good at them. For the most part I stick to them." Suddenly he lifted his head and gave her a searching glance. "Is that going to bother you? I can't change myself completely, honey. In the last analysis, I'm afraid I tend to run my life on an organized basis."

Elly laughed softly. "I'm not worried. Lately you've shown yourself to be highly adaptable." She pulled him close, pushing her leg tantalizingly between his thighs. His low groan of arousal was her immediate reward. When she let her fingertips trail down his chest to the excitingly rough hair below his flat stomach, he groaned again.

Jess reached out and felt the shape of her hip with his hand, letting his fingers sink into her soft, resilient skin. "I'm amazingly adaptable when it comes to making love to you. Haven't you noticed? I didn't really mind the first time you threw off my schedule by trying to seduce me ahead of time. I'll be just as adaptable forty or fifty years from now. A man has to be flexible about some things."

Elly grinned, touching him intimately. "Flexible isn't exactly how I would describe you at the moment."

"I warned you. I told you that if you were going to push a man, you'd have to learn to take the consequences." He rolled over on top of her, pinning her beneath him. The brief humor faded as he felt her wrap herself around him. Gray eyes gleamed in the shadows, and the lines of his harsh face became etched with his hunger.

"I love you, Jess."

"I know," he whispered. "I've never known what it was like to be loved until I met you. I could never let you go now. Do you realize that? I love you so much, Elly. It's such an incredible relief to finally say it."

He moved then, joining his body to hers in a rush of passion that brought with it a sense of forever. Elly didn't question the feeling. She clung to it and to the man who created it. Jess was giving himself completely, just as she had given herself to him. Jess Winter always seemed to know what he was doing.

Take 4
Silhouette Special Edition novels
FREE...

and preview future books in your home for 15 days!

Start with 4 FREE books, yours to keep. Then, preview 6 brand-new Special Edition® novels—delivered right to your door every month—as soon as they are published.

When you decide to keep them, pay just $1.95 each ($2.50 each in Canada), *with no shipping, handling, or other additional charges of any kind!*

Romance *is* alive, well and flourishing in the moving love stories presented by Silhouette Special Edition. They'll awaken your desires, enliven your senses, and leave you tingling all over with excitement. In each romance-filled story you'll live and breathe the emotions of love and the satisfaction of romance triumphant.

You won't want to miss a single one of the heartfelt stories presented by Silhouette Special Edition; and when you take advantage of this special offer, you won't have to.

You'll also receive a FREE subscription to the Silhouette Books Newsletter as long as you remain a member. Each lively issue is filled with news on upcoming titles, interviews with your favorite authors, even their favorite recipes.

To become a home subscriber and receive your first 4 books FREE, fill out and mail the coupon today!

Silhouette Special Edition®

Silhouette Books, 120 Brighton Rd., P.O. Box 5084, Clifton, NJ 07015-5084

Take 4
Silhouette Intimate Moments novels
FREE...

If you're the kind of woman who wants more passion from your romance novels...

... preview 4 brand new Silhouette Intimate Moments® novels—delivered right to your door every month—for 15 days as soon as they are published. When you decide to keep them, you pay just $2.25 each ($2.50 each, in Canada), *with no shipping, handling, or other charges of any kind!*

These romance novels are not for everyone. They were created to give you a more detailed, more exciting reading experience, filled with romantic fantasy...dynamic, contemporary characters... involving stories...intense sensuality and stirring passion.

If that's the kind of romance reading you're looking for, Silhouette Intimate Moments novels were created for you.

The first 4 Silhouette Intimate Moments selections are absolutely FREE and without obligation, yours to keep! You can cancel at any time.

You'll also receive a FREE subscription to the Silhouette Books Newsletter as long as you remain a member. Its filled with news on upcoming books, interviews with your favorite authors, even their favorite recipes.

To get your first 4 Silhouette Intimate Moments novels FREE, fill out and mail the coupon today!

Silhouette Intimate Moments®

Silhouette Books, 120 Brighton Rd., P.O. Box 5084, Clifton, NJ 07015-5084

⚡ Silhouette Desire

COMING
NEXT MONTH

OUT OF THIS WORLD—Janet Joyce
When Adrienne met Kendrick, she thought he was an alien from outer space. He insisted he wasn't, but how could she believe him when his mere touch sent her soaring to the heavens?

DESPERADO—Doreen Owens Malek
Half Seminole Indian, Andrew Fox had chosen the dangerous life of a bounty hunter. As a student of Indian folklore, Cindy found him fascinating—as a woman, she found him irresistible.

PICTURE OF LOVE—Robin Elliott
It didn't take Steve long to realize Jade was the woman for him, but Jade was a compulsive overachiever. Could she manage to temper her ambition and make room for love?

SONGBIRD—Syrie A. Astrahan
Desirée had to choose—her career as a disk jockey in California or Kyle Harrison, the man she loved, in Seattle. Could she possibly find the best of both worlds?

BODY AND SOUL—Jennifer Greene
Joel Brannigan fought for what he wanted, and he wanted Dr. Claire Barrett. She was ready for a fair fight, but Joel didn't fight fair...and he always won.

IN THE PALM OF HER HAND—Dixie Browning
Fate had thrown Shea Bellwood and Dave Pendleton together under rather bizarre circumstances, but who can argue with fate—especially when it leads to love.

AVAILABLE NOW:

CAUTIOUS LOVER
Stephanie James

WHEN SNOW MEETS FIRE
Christine Flynn

HEAVEN ON EARTH
Sandra Kleinschmit

NO MAN'S KISSES
Nora Powers

THE SHADOW BETWEEN
Diana Stuart

NOTHING VENTURED
Suzanne Simms